C000124639

My Grumpy Billionaire Boss

Kathilee Riley

Published by Kathilee Riley, 2023.

Table of Contents

.... 1

Prologue... 3

Chapter 1.. 15

Chapter 2.. 33

Chapter 3.. 39

Chapter 4.. 45

Chapter 5.. 53

Chapter 6.. 63

Chapter 7.. 69

Chapter 8.. 85

Chapter 9.. 97

Chapter 10 107

Chapter 11 113

Chapter 12 119

Chapter 13 127

Chapter 14 135

Chapter 15 143

Chapter 16 153

Chapter 17 163

Chapter 18 169

Chapter 19 175

Chapter 20 181

Chapter 21 189

Chapter 22 195

Epilogue...201

My Grumpy Billionaire Boss: Possessive Alpha CEO

Off-Limits Older Man Younger Woman Age-Gap Romance

Forbidden Daddy Steamy Novels
Kathilee Riley[1]

---

1. _https://www.amazon.com/stores/Kathilee-Riley/author/B0BTCW6HF7_

Prologue

Alyssa

I slid the hotel key into the door, thanking the stars I'd brought enough cash to bribe the front desk clerk. His expression had gone from stern to polite within seconds after I flashed the four fifties in my hand. A quick check of his surroundings and the hard plastic met the center of my palm so discreetly that I almost missed his move. Something told me he'd done this before. No judgement from me, especially after getting what I wanted.

Coming here tonight, I had no real plan, just an endgame; to sneak into my mom's drop-dead gorgeous boss' hotel room and seduce my way into his bed. Piece of cake, considering how often he flirted with me whenever I stopped by Mom's workplace and the many times we'd made out in his office. For two months, I waited for him to hit a home run, but we remained stuck at third base, which was pretty frustrating for an eighteen-year-old with a sky-high libido. Tonight, my only intention was to nudge him to the home plate myself.

It still flattered me that Tony Bancroft even looked my way. Not that I had any self-esteem issues or anything, but I was just a high school graduate with nothing to offer. Sure, I looked a little older than a typical eighteen-year-old with a curvy body to match, but Tony knew my age. What did he want with a girl like me when he could have any woman he wanted?

My best friend Elizabeth said he only wanted a good time, but I didn't believe her. Tony was too affectionate, too caring. There was no way he only wanted my body. If he did, I wouldn't be sneaking into his hotel room to seduce him into making love to me.

I always took Liz's opinion with a grain of salt, anyway. Like how she thought he was too old for me. The twenty-year age gap didn't bother me at all. Boys my age were too immature, too ignorant of how to pleasure me. After wasting so much time with guys in my age group, I now wanted a real man to rock my world.

My cell phone vibrated in my hand as I closed the door behind me. I glanced at the screen with a frown, almost groaning when I saw Mom's name on the screen. No doubt this was a *when-are-you-coming-home* phone call, despite our discussion two days ago about her getting rid of her helicopter-mom behavior and just letting me live. I was now an adult, completely capable of making my own decisions. Granted, I'd been making my own decisions long before then—terrible ones—hence her hovering behavior—but I'd learned from my mistakes.

No more using sex as a distraction.

No more getting high to mask my pain.

No more partying—no, scratch that. I couldn't live without reveling and alcohol, especially with college only two weeks away. I smiled, thinking of the exciting time ahead.

Swiping the screen to cut the call, I sent Mom a short message, letting her know I was out with Liz and would be home by midnight. Not true since Liz was all the way in New York with her new boyfriend, and I had no plans to leave Tony's bed until the morning. Quite a confident assumption, but I had good reason. I paused by the floor-to-ceiling mirror on the wall and assessed my curvy figure in the loose dress I wore, loving how it gave my short legs a lengthy illusion. My dark hair hung in waves over my shoulders, framing my round face embellished by rosy cheeks and soft hazel eyes. On the surface, I looked like an innocent young woman, but deep inside, I was no sweetheart. The devil groaned whenever he heard me coming. At least, that's what my mom always said.

I wasn't always like that, sneaking off to be with boys, partying every weekend, underage drinking and driving while under the influence. But after my dad died in a car accident three years ago, I tried doing everything to numb the hurt. Nothing worked, which left me angry and rebellious, wanting to lash out in every way. Until Tony came into the picture, and for some reason, it made me want to change.

Maybe it was the way he attended to me; like, he really *listened* when I talked about my issues. He saw *me*. Unlike Mom, who brushed aside my pain, telling me how lucky I was to have a roof over my head, not having to worry about money, etc. I got it. Dad's insurance ensured we could live comfortably for a little while, but didn't *she* get it? It wasn't enough. There was a void that needed filling. I wanted nothing more than to feel normal again.

With a deep sigh, I moved away from the mirror, placing my phone on the night table. The sound of the running shower hit my ears, resurrecting my smile. The gloom faded away as I removed my dress, pulling the duvet aside and climbing into the king-sized bed. Thank God I wore no bra or panties. It made undressing so much quicker.

And within the right time, too.

No sooner had I pulled the sheet over my breasts than the shower stopped running. I fluffed my hair a little, hoping it gave that sexy, tousled look. With my shoulders squared and with what I hoped was an alluring smile, I waited for Tony to enter the bedroom.

But as the bathroom door opened, the smile slipped from my face. This wasn't Tony. There was a dark-haired, scary-looking giant standing in his place.

My body instantly froze when the stranger stepped from the darkness, coming to an abrupt stop when he saw me. His hand gripped the front of the towel wrapped around his hips, beads of water decorating his muscular torso.

His thick lashes blinked furiously as if trying to determine if the image before him was real. Shock still kept me frozen to the spot. I wanted to speak, but no words emerged.

The giant moved closer, his dark eyes carrying a hint of fury. "Who the fuck are you?" he demanded, his tone thick and deep, perfectly matching his huge frame, thawing me out.

"I—I—um..." It wasn't an actual response but better than nothing.

"Young lady, you'd better speak up right now before I call hotel security. What the fuck are you doing in my room?" His face was now tight with the fury that filled his voice.

A flutter of fear crept up my spine as realization set in. Here I was with nothing but a sheet covering my nakedness and a total stranger—a huge stranger—standing in front of me, a man who could overpower me without breaking a sweat. Too late, my mom's warnings came back at me, and I didn't know what to do with myself. I was at his mercy, and if he had none, whatever happened from now on would be my fault.

The stranger pivoted from me with a deep groan, stomping over to the landline on the night table. When I realized what he was about to do, I threw the covers aside and scampered from bed, forgetting I had no clothes on.

"Wait!" I called out.

He whipped to me, freezing for an instant, then pivoting again. "For fuck's sake, put some clothes on."

Shame twisted my insides as I reached for my dress on the floor. "I'm sorry, but please don't call hotel security. My mom can't know about this."

He paused, holding the phone in midair, twisting his head to glance back at me. His shoulders relaxed when he saw me fully dressed, my nervous hands smoothing the sides of my dress.

"Your mom? How old are you?" he asked.

"Um..." His penetrating stare made my lips falter with the lie, but I still proceeded. "Twenty," I replied.

His eyes did a quick scan of my body, leaving me wondering if he noticed I had no panties on. Was my dress see-through?

Without a word, he returned the phone to the cradle and turned back to me. I breathed an inaudible sigh of relief.

"Who are you, and what are you doing in my room?" he asked, his tone softer this time.

I straightened my posture. "I– I..."

A slight smirk pulled the corner of his lips apart. "I didn't peg you as a shy girl, considering..." his voice trailed as he gestured to the rumpled bed.

For some reason, his response sent me in defense mode, and I narrowed my eyes at him, my hands flying to my hips. "My name is Alyssa, and for your information, I'm not an escort. There's obviously been a mix-up."

"I didn't say you were an escort, but can you explain how this mix-up happened?"

"I had plans to meet someone here," I replied. "Clearly, I have the wrong room."

He stepped closer, filling the space between us with his fresh-from-the-shower scent, rosewood mixed with another flavor I couldn't identify. It made me feel warm and cozy and... weird.

"Which means you have the wrong key. I should call the front desk and have them rectify the issue."

"No!" I screamed, and his thick brows shot up at me. The last thing I wanted was for the front desk clerk to lose his job on my behalf. "Don't do that."

His lips curled into a knowing smile. "Because you bribed the staff out front, didn't you?"

"I'm not answering that," I replied defiantly.

"No need. The answer's already in your eyes. Which means whoever you planned to meet had no idea you were coming, am I right?"

I didn't answer.

He tapped his finger against his chin, looking upwards as if thinking. "Considering I switched places with my colleague at the last minute, I'm now wondering if he was your intended target slash victim, am I right?"

"I don't know what you're talking about."

"Mmh." A sparkle filled his eyes, giving him a boyish look that made him even more attractive. "You snuck in to see Tony Bancroft, didn't you?" he asked.

I hugged my shoulder, the gentle gasp leaving my mouth before I could stop it. The spark disappeared, immediately replaced by a steely gaze that held me in place. "Fucking hell, Tony," he muttered to himself. "I thought you were done with this shit."

"Where is Tony?" I asked, brushing his comment aside. I'd overheard his assistant booking this room on his behalf last week to prepare for his keynote speech in the hotel ballroom tomorrow. He had to be in the building somewhere.

The stranger scoffed. "You don't want to know, believe me."

My heart dipped as I processed his shady response. This wasn't good. Not at all.

"Where is he?" I asked again.

"Don't push it, little girl." The warning came out in a low growl, but instead of putting me on edge, it awakened a stirring inside me. Why did those five words make me want to fan myself?

He dipped, coming to my level, fixing me with a hard stare. "Let. It. Go."

"I can't. Tell me, please." I didn't intend to whisper, but the words left my mouth in a gentle hiss, the stranger's gaze dropping to my lips. His chest heaved as he uttered a low curse. He dragged a hand through his damp hair and moved toward the door.

"You've overstayed your welcome. Time to go," he said.

"Listen. I'm a big girl. I can handle the truth," I replied, following him.

The stranger paused with his hand on the doorknob, amusement dancing in his eyes. "Are you sure about that?"

"Positive."

"Fine. Tony's in Las Vegas getting hitched." He glanced at the wall clock beside us. "Yup. Probably done the deed by now."

My body went rigid. "What do you mean by hitched?"

A flash of pity crossed his face before his expression hardened. "Tony got *married*, little girl. His fiancée didn't want to wait for an elaborate wedding, so he took her to Vegas. The best decision, if you ask me."

"Fiancée?" The single word came out breathlessly as his words resonated with me.

"You heard me," he said.

I did, but I didn't want to believe his words were true.

"He had a girlfriend?" I asked, my gaze now searching the carpeted floor.

"A *fiancée*," he elaborated.

Tears pricked my eyes. Somehow, during Tony's flirting, the many times we made out in his office and the backseat of his car, he never once relayed that fact to me. During those times, with his hand up my skirt giving me pleasure, he told me I was the one. He promised me forever. How could he do this to me?

"Listen, I hate to be the bearer of bad news, but sweetheart, you're not the first. Based on how reckless Tony's been, you probably won't be the last. Chalk this down as a life lesson and go home to your mother. You're not ready for this kind of heat, anyway."

"You don't know me. Don't tell me what I can't handle," I replied defiantly, despite the tears rolling down my cheeks.

Again, his eyes did that full-motion scan of my figure that left me feeling exposed, and my mind rebelled against my body's satisfaction from the attraction in his eyes. He took obvious pleasure in my demise, and I disliked him for that. Did he not understand how embarrassing this was for me?

He closed the remaining distance between us, filling me with an awareness of him. Every inch of his torso met my direct gaze; his thick pecs and arms, flat torso, the sexy V that created the juncture between his thighs, barely covered by that towel. My eyes dropped a little lower, and my mouth flew open when I saw the unmistakable bulge there. Holy shit, he was aroused. For me. I should be scared. I should run. My only reaction was to lick my lips.

I heard a soft rumble from his lips before he stepped aside, gesturing to the door. "Run home, little girl. Tony used the shit out of you. For your sake, I hope he didn't fuck you because all you'd be is another notch on his belt. Another stupid mistake."

"You're such an asshole," I sniffled, burned by his comment.

"And you're a desperate, naïve girl who needs a wake-up call. You snuck into a stranger's hotel room, for fuck's sake. What if Tony had asked someone dangerous to take his place instead? You could've been hurt, or worse—"

"I didn't know, okay?" I shouted. "Don't stand there acting all self-righteous, like you've never made a mistake in your life."

"Not if I can help it," he replied. "And nothing as stupid as this."

My lips trembled as I stood there, wanting to move but trying to find a cutting response. The only thing that left my mouth was, "Okay, Mr. Perfect, I hope you never make a mistake for as long as you live."

He waved aside my response wearily. "Go away. Now."

I finally broke into a fit of sobs, blurring the image of this beastly man who stood unmoving as I broke down. With a sniff and the swift brush of my tears, I bolted out of the room and ran into the elevator, grateful when the doors closed at once. I wanted no one to see my tears. My shame was already too great. I kept my head down as I crossed the lobby, opting to walk for a while to clear my head.

What should've been the perfect night spent in the arms of the man of my dreams had turned out to be the most shameful night ever. I winced, recalling the disgust on the stranger's face when he connected the dots. In his eyes, I was nothing but a slut, and he wasn't far off the mark.

My cellphone beeped with an alert, and I checked the screen. It was an Instagram notification. Nothing worth reading. As I made to lock the phone, the screensaver caught my eye. It was a photo of me and Dad a few months before he died. Fresh tears filled my eyes as I stopped, staring at the photo. Back then, life was so simple. I was such a good kid. I made the honor roll every year, did all my chores, made curfew. Everything changed in the blink of an eye because of a careless driver.

For the first time in three years, I reflected on my actions. Sleeping around for the heck of it, living on the edge with recreational drugs, drinking until I passed out...this wasn't the life I wanted to live. It certainly wasn't the life Dad wanted for me.

I sank down on a bench near the docks, sobs racking my body when I thought of my dad and how he'd be ashamed of me, how he'd agree with everything the stranger said. In trying to numb the pain from his loss, I became a girl he wouldn't recognize if he came back. I didn't want to be that girl anymore. I wanted to make him proud.

"Oh, Daddy," I breathed, throwing my head back on the seat and staring at the starlit sky, the residue of tears running out the corners of my eyes. "I miss you!"

I closed my eyes, remembering the happy days. A knot formed in my chest as the image of Mom's unhappy face crossed my mind. I wasn't the only one suffering grief from losing Dad, and for three years, I'd selfishly taken center stage. Not once did I consider Mom's feelings. Instead, I made her grief even worse.

Reaching for my phone, I dialed her number, and she answered on the first ring. "Sweetie, are you okay?"

The concern in her voice triggered a fresh round of tears. I pressed my fingers to my temple, the force of my crying giving me a headache.

"Alyssa?"

"I'm on my way home, Mom. Just letting you know. And I'm sorry for everything."

"Oh, honey. Hurry home. We'll talk when you get here, okay?"

I returned the phone to my purse as I rose from the seat, and I glanced at the starlit sky before moving off. "I'm going to do my best from now on, Dad. I promise."

Chapter 1

Alyssa

Five Years Later

It amazed me how I once thought school was a total nightmare, and I often cringed when I remembered the days I skipped school to hang out with other wayward kids and smoke pot. But, after spending the last five years working on myself, I didn't recognize that rebellious girl anymore. In fact, she no longer existed. Alyssa Reynolds was now a college graduate with a first-class finance degree.

For five years I'd kept my head down. No partying, no drinking, just focused on school; then, after graduation, I spent a year working for a non-profit organization involved with feeding the homeless. It paid little, but it left me feeling so fulfilled, I would've continued if Mom didn't suddenly need me at home.

"Sweetie, do you need help getting your stuff to your room?" Mom asked, cutting me from my musing.

Pausing at the foot of the stairs, I shook my head while tightening my grip on the handles of my suitcases. "No, Mom, I've got this."

Halfway up the stairs, I heard her say, "It's good to have you back, Honey."

I turned and gave her a soft smile, then continued upwards. The feeling wasn't a mutual one. I didn't want to come back home. After living in Washington D.C. for five years and only coming home for the holidays, the awful memories of my past eventually faded. Now, I feared a permanent move back home would only resurrect them once more. The pain from losing Dad, the regret from all the bullshit I'd done back in high school, and the shame from my crazy attempt to seduce my mom's boss... I didn't want to face them again. If only Mom didn't need me as much.

I blew a deep sigh as I dumped the luggage on my bedroom floor and moved to my window, lifting the sill to let the air in. The room remained exactly how I'd left it when I'd come home last Christmas, except for the fluffy pink sheets that now covered the queen-sized bed. The closet still contained the skimpy outfits I'd left behind, stuff I'd discard the minute I settled down. I walked over to the dresser, lifting a bottle of my favorite perfume and taking a sniff. To be honest, after living in a small apartment with three roommates, I missed having my own private space. If only I could move it somewhere else.

Returning the perfume to its place, I walked back to the window, taking in the view of the garden below. After Mom paid my college tuition in full, money was now really tight. I applied for full-time jobs back in D.C., but the market was too competitive, forcing me to return home when the rent was too much to bear. As much as I didn't want to be here, there was no doubt I'd find a job in no time, even outside my field.

A knock came at the door, and I eased my head out the window as it creaked open. My mom's head poked through, a tentative smile on her face.

"Hey, honey," she said, pushing the door further open and stepping inside.

I managed a smile. "Hey, Mom."

She pulled in a breath as she walked toward me with her fingers intertwined in front of her.

"Everything okay?" I asked, seeing the worry on her face.

Mom took a seat beside me, forcing me to meet her emerald gaze. "You'd been so quiet on the drive back from the airport. Now, you're locked in your room after barely saying two words to me. I'm starting to get concerned," she softly said.

I gave her hand a reassuring squeeze. At least, I hoped it was. "I'm just trying to figure out the next step, Mom," I replied.

"I know, honey, but you don't have to worry about it too much. You're still young, barely out of college a year now. It's fine if you take some more time to have some fun and relax before you start thinking about anything else."

I shook my head. "There's no time for fun, Mom. Didn't you tell me how tough things are? There's the mortgage, utilities, insurance—you can't do this on your own anymore. It's time for me to pitch in. I need to start sending out my resume so I can help bear the burden."

Mom stared at me for a short beat, awe filling her face.

"What?" I asked.

"Who are you, and what have you done with my feisty, rebellious child?"

I chuckled. "I grew up, Mom. It took moving away to college to make me realize how big of an asshole I was."

"You weren't an asshole. You were in pain."

"So were you, and you didn't do anything outrageous, like sleep with half the town." I peered at her closely. "Did you?"

Mom laughed. "We both know I didn't. Don't beat yourself up over a silly mistake, sweetie. You've clearly learned from it, so move on. Have fun."

"No time for fun," I repeated.

"You know, it's strange for me to admit this, but I miss the girl you were back in high school. So carefree and living life one day at a time, having fun..."

I shot her a skeptical stare. "Mom—"

"I'm not saying you should be that irresponsible or rebellious, but I just wished you worried less now as you did then."

"There's nothing wrong with worrying sometimes. It keeps me on my toes."

She clasped my cheeks with her hands. "Ally, you're still young. You have plenty of time to worry about life, especially when it gets really shitty. Promise me you won't let our situation get to your head. Promise me you'll let your hair down and live a little."

I smiled, covering her hands with mine. "I promise, Mom."

"Now, get some rest. I imagine Liz will be thrilled to know you're back. Call her later, won't you? Maybe go out for drinks, get your weekend started..."

"Sounds like fun," I replied, the first wave of excitement running through me. I hadn't seen Liz since Thanksgiving, and although we kept in contact, Facetime and text messaging couldn't replace seeing her in person.

Mom smiled and leaned down, kissing my forehead. "Great, I have some overtime to do, so I'm heading back to the office."

I raised a brow at her. "It's a Saturday."

She sighed. "I know, but we have a new CEO, and I want to get on his good side, which is a hard feat, I might add. I've never seen a man so intense."

"Intense?" I asked.

"It's an understatement, actually. I think he has a permanent stick up his ass—don't mention a word of this to anyone, by the way," she warned, pointing at me. She continued after I pressed my finger to my lips. "He never smiles. Ever. Not even when we broke the profit margin during the first quarter. Anyone who puts a toe out of line gets fired in a heartbeat. He works long hours, and although he hasn't explicitly ordered us to do the same, no one dares leave early, for fear they won't have a job the next day."

"Gosh, that's awful," I replied. "I can imagine how hellish the work environment must be."

"It's not hell, just a distant cousin. Still, I miss having Tony Bancroft as a boss. You remember Tony, don't you?"

With a wince I hoped she didn't notice, I nodded in reply.

"Such a pity when the board asked for his resignation. There were rumors it was over sexual misconduct at the office, but I'd never seen the signs. He was always such a gentleman toward me."

Because you were way too old for him, that's why, I wanted to say, but I kept my mouth shut as she continued.

"Tony was a smart man. I doubt he'd throw away his career for sex, especially with such a beautiful wife."

Double wince. I kicked off my sneakers, pulling back the covers on the bed. "Think I'm going to take that nap, Mom," I announced.

"Okay, honey, get some rest," she replied, ruffling my hair before moving toward the door.

I waited for the door to close, then reached for my phone, my thumb lingering over the screen as I pondered my Mom's advice. Maybe she was right; I needed to go out and have some fun. I'd finished college with honors, which was a freaking huge deal. Perfect cause for celebration. A belated one, I might add.

Excitement filled me as I dialed Liz's number, biting my lips as I waited for a reply. I had many friends in high school, but Liz was the only one who kept in touch during college. Apparently, my good-girl vibe was too much for them. They wanted the wild Alyssa to show up for spring break, but all they got was the watered-down version who stood in a corner at the parties sipping water from a bottle. I'd never been invited out since then. Not that I minded. I was already on the road to changing my life.

"Well, hello there, Miss D.C!" Liz answered, her high-pitched voice making me pull away the phone from my ear. "Please tell me you're finally home."

"Yup. Unfortunately," I murmured.

"What's that supposed to mean?"

I shook my head, although she couldn't see me. "Nothing. How have you been?"

"Busy enjoying life. Just got back from a weekend in Ibiza. Girl, I'm still hungover." She giggled. "I'm still high, too."

"I guess that means I'm flying solo tonight. Thought I'd hit the club or something."

There was a loud gasp on Liz's end. "Did you say club?"

"Yes, I did."

Another gasp. "Who are you, and what have you done with my best friend?"

"Don't be a drama queen, Liz," I said, chuckling.

"No, seriously. I never expected to hear those words coming from your mouth ever again."

"I turned over a new page. It doesn't mean I'm a prude. I can do clubbing, even a little drinking, as long as it doesn't get out of hand."

"Okay! I love how this sounds! Name a place, and I'll be there."

"There's a new club on the other side of town I'd always wanted to go. I'll text you the address. Say, around ten? How does that sound?" I asked.

"Sounds great. I'll see you then."

I ended the call and settled in bed before browsing social media, lingering on Instagram since I liked to keep track of my old schoolmates. Most were still waist-deep in post-college celebrations, with nightclub photos, trips to exotic destinations and tons of foam parties decorating my timeline. I sighed as I browsed, a part of me envying them for being so free. But, sometimes, I wished the old me would emerge. Even for a moment.

My fingers paused on a familiar face, my stomach churning as I stared at the beautiful family photo with the unmistakable swell of the woman's belly. They both wore hundred-watt smiles, their happiness and the caption announcing their most recent pregnancy making me sick.

Stupid Alyssa. Did you really think this man loved you?

My insides churned whenever I thought of our affair, and like every other time, I mentally slapped myself for being so stupid. To think I thought he cared for me. The asshole had never even called to apologize for leading me on.

With shaky fingers, I hastily clicked on his profile and unfollowed him, then threw my phone beside me, something I should've done long ago, but I needed a reminder every now and then of how reckless I'd been. It also motivated me to never backslide again.

The old Alyssa, that impulsive girl who broke all the rules was gone, never to return, and I vowed to do everything in my power to keep her buried. Good Girl Alyssa was here to stay.

After realizing sleep would not come, I peeled myself out of bed and moved to my closet for something to wear tonight.

A HONK OUTSIDE ALERTED me to Liz's arrival. Just in time since I was just about ready, anyway. I used my hand to smoothen my short bodycon dress before I gave myself one final twirl in the mirror and headed out.

My midsize heels clicked on the stairs as I descended to find Mom curled up on the couch with a glass of wine. Not good. Mom only drank when she got upset, which was rare.

"Oh-oh," I say, stopping in front of her. "Who's the asshole who pissed you off?"

Mom sighed, twirling the stem of the glass. "I'm not upset, just a little flustered."

"They kinda mean the same thing, Mom," I teased, and she snickered.

"Whatever, Miss Honorary Degree."

"Yes, put that title on my name, Mom. I earned it," I joked.

She laughed, then looked at me tenderly. "It's great to see you in a good mood. I'm not so worried anymore."

I sat beside her. "Liz and I are heading out, and it's already doing wonders for my spirit."

"Good for you," she replied.

"Now, tell me what got you so flustered."

"Work stuff, honey. Nothing to concern yourself about."

"Did you have a fight with your boss or something?"

She shook her head. "Not a fight. He's just really scary sometimes."

I stared at my mom, surprised that anything could scare her after everything she'd gone through. Her boss sounded like a monster. A far cry from Tony—

No. I won't think about him.

Liz's horn tooted impatiently, making me jump. "Go on, honey. Don't keep Liz waiting any longer," Mom said.

I gave her a quick peck on her cheek before heading out. Liz's brand new, red convertible stood in the driveway, just as shiny as its owner. Her sparkly dress and the grin on her face put me in a festive mood as I slipped onto the front seat. She eyed me up and down, her expression telling me she approved of my look.

"I hope the fire department is on standby. You look just about ready to burn shit down."

I grinned, running my finger along her figure. "I'm not the only one."

We briefly hugged before she reversed out the driveway, her blonde hair dancing in the wind as she pressed gas and cranked up the radio.

"God, I want to get so fucked up tonight!" she shouted over the bass in the car.

My face scrunched, and I gripped the handle of the car door. "I'll settle for mild tipsy, thank you," I replied, not feeling as enthusiastic as her.

She glanced at me, a wrinkle in her forehead, before she leaned forward and turned down the music. "Listen, Ally, I know you've been turning over a new leaf and all, which I commend, but there's nothing wrong with letting down your hair tonight. Get wasted, dance with a few guys. Just let yourself go. Please."

I smiled. "I'll try."

"And who knows? You just might find Mr. Right tonight."

"Mr. Right?" I twisted in the seat to stare at her. "How did we go from having fun to finding the one?"

She shrugged. "I figured that was your endgame. You know, with you switching to good girl mode and all."

"I'm not even thinking about a man, Liz. Seriously. I haven't gotten laid since high school."

Liz's sudden braking had me flying against the dashboard. "Liz! What the fuck?"

"What did you just say?" she asked, her hair covering half of her face.

"I said what the fuck? Why did you brake like that?"

"I meant before that."

I searched my thoughts. "I haven't been laid since high school."

"You're lying!"

"No, for real, though. I've been so focused on school; I had no time to even hook up."

"Hence that first class degree. Proud of you, by the way, but sweetie, those cobwebs must be getting to you by now."

She laughed as I punched her arm. "Seriously, Ally. You're done with college. It's time to stop acting like a forty-year-old woman, have some fun! Are you with me?"

"Right there with you, Liz," I replied as she shook my shoulder.

"Awesome sauce." She turned the volume up again, her foot heavy on the gas pedal once more.

Feeling my excitement return, I threw my hands in the air, rocking to the music as we cruised our way downtown.

SINCE LIZ WAS THE DAUGHTER of Anthony Abel, a popular architect, it wasn't hard getting into the club without joining the depressingly long line outside. The club was already in full swing, bodies gyrating on the over-packed dance floor to a Hip-Hop beat that pounded my ears. Five years ago, the loud music wouldn't have bothered me one bit, but now all I wanted to do was plug my ears and make a U-turn, heading right back home. I fought against the urge, knowing my best friend had made a valid point earlier. I'd done good by turning my life around, and there was no harm in loosening up a bit.

It took me a moment to realize Liz had moved off, and I followed, bumping against bodies as I made my way through the crowd. I caught up with her at the bar, where she greeted a few friends I recognized from high school.

"You remember Kayla and Alex, right?"

I gave a gentle wave to the striking brunette and the tall, good-looking guy, who smiled back at me. "Of course," I replied, my gaze traveling down Kayla's skin-tight dress. "You look amazing, Kayla."

"You're one to talk!" Kayla exclaimed, sweeping her hands down my frame. "That dress was so made for you. And those heels! Good to know you're still keeping up. Liz told me you're a bookworm now and everything."

"A sexy bookworm," Alex added, raising his tumbler at me.

"You know what, Alex? I'm going to own that. Sexy bookworm it is," I replied with a laugh.

"What are you having, girl?" Liz asked, gently nudging my side, the bartender patiently waiting for our order.

"A dry martini—shaken, not stirred."

Liz grinned. "Welcome back, Ally! I thought you would order a chocolate milkshake or something."

I grinned back, shoving her shoulder. She gave the bartender our order, and I took a seat at the counter, watching the patrons on the dance floor. The dim lights weren't enough to hide the sensual bumping and grinding, hands groping, full-blown make-out sessions happening in front of me. My body came alive, arousal stirring me, and I shifted uncomfortably on the seat as I looked on, so caught up with the carnal exchanges I didn't notice Liz poking my side.

"Hey," she said as I blinked at her. "Where'd you go?"

"Just watching the dance floor," I replied, gesturing with my chin.

"Sexy, isn't it?" She handed me the drink. "One step away from fucking in public, if you ask me."

"How about we quit being bystanders and actually join in?" Alex suggested, and we agreed, following him into the crowd.

The music switched to an alternative mix—much more my style— and in no time, we were having the time of our lives, bouncing and screaming as I entered that place of freedom where nothing mattered to me but having fun. Liz, Kayla and Alex were the best dance companions, their high energy so infectious. Sweat poured from my face, running down my body by the time the first round of songs was over. I couldn't keep the smile off my face, but soon enough, something did when I realized I needed another drink.

"I'll be back," I announced before I made my way through the crowd that had gotten even thicker since we'd been here.

I smiled at the bartender, who spotted me coming, and he winked, pausing from wiping the counter as I approached, my focus directly on him. I was almost there when someone slammed into me, followed by the cold splash of something against my chest. I gasped and stepped back, staring down at my wet cleavage and the overpowering smell of beer that filled my nostrils.

With my mouth still wide open in shock, I glared at the offender, a good-looking guy about my age. His wide blue eyes looked down on me, his hand still awkwardly holding the half-spilled beer. His Adam's apple bobbed as his gaze dropped lower, stopping at my cleavage.

"Seriously?" I snapped. "My eyes are up here, asshole."

He shook his head as if trying to clear it, his eyes popping up to my face. "My bad," he muttered. "This happens when I run across a beautiful woman, you know?"

I rolled my eyes at him. "You're corny as hell. Next time, watch where you're going!"

"Next time, don't wear that dress," he threw back. "That's another accident waiting to happen."

I flipped my middle finger at him and was about to walk off when he said, "At least let me buy you a drink to make up for it."

"Worry about your own drink," I said, smirking at the half-spilled mug in his hand. I made my way to the counter, ignoring the feel of his eyes on me.

Huffing an annoyed breath, I slipped onto an empty barstool, reaching for a napkin on the counter and dabbing at my chest, hating the cold, sticky feeling I now had to deal with.

"I feel horrible about that mess," his voice came from behind me. "Let me buy you a drink. I won't take no for an answer."

With my hands curled into fists, I turned to glare at him, yet couldn't help but acknowledge how attractive he was, his dark hair mussed at the top and faded at the sides. His face was clean-shaved – not even a stubble in sight – giving him a friendly, boyish look.

"Well if you insist," I conceded. "I'll have another dry martini please."

He smiled, revealing a line of pearly whites. "Good choice," he commented before turning to the bartender and placing the order along with a beer for himself. He turned back to me with a hand outstretched, the other brushing stray locks from his face. "I'm Blake... Blake Kinley."

I stared down at his hand before finally placing mine in his. "Alyssa."

"Lovely name, Alyssa. It's nice to meet you."

I stared down at my stained dress. "I think you understand why I can't say the same."

He sighed, remorse filling his face. "Again, I'm sorry about that. Typical me. Met the most beautiful girl in the club and had to ruin it."

I bit my lips, assessing him. "You have a way with words, don't you?"

"Just being honest," he replied with a shrug. "You are a beautiful woman, Alyssa."

"Flattery will get you anywhere, I guess. Only if this were wine you'd spilled on my dress, I'd have your balls in a vice grip right now."

His eyes widened, then he relaxed as I chuckled. "You look like you would actually kill someone who ruined such a perfect dress – no offense... of course, you don't look like a killer. Killers aren't always this attractive..." he trailed off and raked his fingers through his hair. "Fuck, I don't know why I'm suddenly so nervous."

I took him in, the buttoned shirt done all the way to his collar, neatly groomed hair and nails, perfect jeans, and a pair of sneakers on his feet. Something told me he wasn't the smooth-talking player he tried to be. It flattered me that he wanted to put on a front for me.

I forced myself from laughing aloud, but I couldn't help my grin. "You're acting all nervous, but it's cute."

His face reddened with a blush, which proved me right.

"I wondered what took you so long," Liz's voice came from my right. I glanced at her as she approached us, her gaze latched onto Blake. "Now I see why." She winked at me, giving an obvious thumbs-up sign.

I pursed my lips at her. "This is Blake, who drenched me with his beer just moments ago. He bought me a martini to make up for it."

"Only a martini?" Liz exclaimed, palming her hips and glaring at Blake. "You ruined her dress, dude. You should buy her a new one, or she'll sue. Don't make me call our lawyer!"

I smiled calmly as Blake's eyes widened, his mouth opening and closing as he looked between us. "I—I—"

"I'm just fucking with you," Liz joked, then burst out laughing.

I gestured between them. "Blake, this is my best friend, Liz—"

"Elizabeth Abel... of course!" He said in awe. "Your dad built half the city."

Liz managed a tight smile at the mention of her dad. I could almost read her thoughts. As much as she loved spending her father's money, she'd rather have him around, but Anthony Abel was too busy conquering the world to spend time with his only child.

"Yeah, listen, Ally, Kayla isn't feeling too good, so I'm gonna drop her home. Alex is still on the dance floor, trying to score a one-night stand." She glanced at Blake, then back at me. "Are you coming or staying?"

"Of course, I'm coming," I replied, turning to Blake. "See you around, Blake. Thanks for the martini... and the beer," I said, looking down at my dress. I winked at his red face before I got up and followed behind Liz.

"Don't mention it!" Blake called to my back, his delayed response making me smile.

"Still into guys twice your age, or are you finally settling for our age group?" Liz asked as we exited the club. Kayla walked ahead, talking to someone on her phone.

I shrugged. "The jury's still out, I guess."

Liz snorted, raising a brow. "Is it? After that disaster with he-who-must-not-be named, do you really think that's a wise choice?"

"Don't remind me about that dick, please."

"Maybe I should." She paused, staring at me sternly, which made me stop, too. "There are plenty of guys our age you can date, Ally. Leave the older men. They're too complicated for you."

"Liz—"

"Luckily for you, that embarrassment with Tony happened behind closed doors with a stranger you'll never see again. Next time, you might not be so lucky. Quit while you're ahead."

"You're talking as if I'm involved with anyone. Give me a break. My only focus is on finding a job and helping Mom out. But—" I pointed at her frowning face. "When I decide to date again, whoever I choose will be my decision. Mine alone!"

"Got it." Liz raised her hands. "Sheesh, no need to be so intense."

I softened my voice, taking her hand. "Sorry... it's just the terrible memories, that's all. I'll never put myself in that position again, I promise. The next man I fall for will be totally mine, not a secret."

"Atta girl," Liz replied, patting my back as we moved off again. "You deserve a man who'll be proud to show you off to the world. Anything else deserves a blatant fuck off, no apologies."

"None whatsoever," I murmured as Liz pulled out from the parking lot.

Chapter 2

Alyssa

Sitting in bed with my legs tucked underneath me, I pressed 'send' on an email of a job application as my mom entered the room with a tentative smile. I gave her a puzzled stare as she joined me.

"What's up?" I asked.

"I see you took my advice. I heard you giggling when you came home last night," she replied.

"Yeah, Liz and I had crazy fun. I'm glad I listened to you. But what's up with that look on your face?"

"Awesome! What are you up to now?" she asked, gesturing to my laptop, clearly avoiding my question."

"Mom..."

She leaned in, reading the content on the laptop screen. "Sending out job applications, I see—"

"Mom!"

"Okay, okay. I have some... news. Just hear me out for a second."

I put the laptop aside and gave her my full attention, watching as she tucked her legs under her.

"What is it?" I asked.

"Do you remember Lorraine Fisher? She's the HR director at work." At my nod, she continued. "She called me last night, just regular conversation, which soon led to us talking about our boss; then Lorraine mentioned he's looking for a temporary assistant. His full-time assistant went off on maternity leave last week, so he's desperate. I pitched in a word, and Lorraine's ready to hire you." She grinned excitedly, briefly clapping her hands together.

I huffed out a breath. "Mom, I have a first-class degree in finance. I'm not interested in serving coffee to some cranky old snob," I said as I rolled my eyes.

She gasped. "He's not a cranky old snob– okay, fine, he's ill-tempered and demanding – but honey, this job pays well, and it could open doors to your true career. Mr. Madden has great connections. If you perform well, who knows what other doors he might open for you."

"That's the thing, Mom. I don't want anyone to open doors for me when I have my own hand."

She sighed heavily. "Well, the reality is, this is how the world works, sweetheart. Very few people leave college and immediately find their dream job. Some never do, plus this is a temporary position. You won't be there forever, but with Stag Technologies being the first thing on your résumé, it'll be a good start; trust me."

"No thanks," I murmured, picking up my laptop.

"You know, honey, I love how independent you are, but this is not that time, not with such a huge opportunity staring in your face."

I fiddled with the keyboard, not knowing what else to say.

"Think about it," she said before getting up and leaving the room.

I rubbed my face with my hands and groaned, feeling flustered for some reason. Although Mom made a good point,

I didn't want to be a temp to her boss. From what she'd told me, he sounded like a nightmare to work with. There were more appealing jobs around.

But, ugh... Executive Assistant—temporary— would certainly look good on my resume. Although *Stag Technologies* had fallen from grace in recent years, they were still ranked high in the industry.

With a huff, I dragged myself from bed and headed downstairs, where I found mom out back by the pool, a glass of wine in hand.

"Isn't it a bit too early for that?" I asked, checking the time. It was a little past twelve.

Mom seemed taken off guard and immediately cleared her throat. "Well, I drank coffee earlier, if that's any consolation," she said, placing the glass on the side table.

"I always remember you scolding Dad on his drinking habits," I said as I took a seat on the opposite end of the table.

"Well, that was before I realized how stressful his job was."

"I bet it's not easy being the head of an IT department either. Must be pretty stressful."

"It can be, but it's what I love."

"I know."

She reached for my hand and gave it a gentle squeeze. "And someday, you'll find a job that you love as well."

I nodded. "I'm going to do the interview, Mom. You were right. I've gotta start somewhere, even if it means being a temp for a back-breaking snob."

Mom frowned at me.

"Sorry. Temp to an ill-tempered CEO."

"Hey, now that you're agreeing to the interview, that description stays here, okay?" Mom said seriously, and I nodded.

"Got it."

Her face brightened with a smile. "Great. Lorraine will want to meet you tomorrow at eight."

I swallowed. "What if I'm not what he's looking for?"

"Trust me, honey, you are. You're intelligent and smarter than you give yourself credit for."

I smiled before I heaved a sigh. "Well, I'd better go and look for something decent to wear."

AFTER CHOOSING MY OUTFIT for the interview, I powered on my laptop, intending to research my potential workplace. Stag Technologies was still a huge deal in the IT industry, so it was no surprise they popped up at the top of the Google search results. As I clicked on the first link that led to their website, my cell phone rang. Seeing Liz's name on the screen made me answer at once, always up to chatting with my best friend.

"Hey, you," I answered. "What's up?"

"Hey, love. It's a Sunday night...up for a little bar hopping?" she asked.

"I'm afraid I can't. I have a job interview tomorrow, and I don't want to mess it up with a hangover," I explained.

"An interview? That's awesome. Where?"

"Stag Technologies. The CEO needs a temp until his assistant returns from maternity leave," I replied glumly.

"Ok... um, a little sound advice, hon, work on that enthusiasm for that interview, okay? At least pretend you actually want the job."

"That's not it, Liz. I can't put my finger on it, but I don't have a good feeling about this. Add to the fact it's not even in my job bracket. I'm a finance major, not some glorified slave."

"I understand how you feel but look at it this way. Stag is a multibillion-dollar company, which would look great on your resume. Think of the doors that connection can open for you."

I sighed. "Just like Mom, you have a point."

"Of course, I do," she said haughtily. "Just try it. The worse thing that can happen is being rejected in that interview, which will never happen, considering how smart and sharp you are. That job is yours, Ally. Go get it."

I couldn't help my smile. "I'm flattered you believe in me."

"Always, bestie. Good luck. I'm gonna hit up Kayla and Alex and see what they're up to since you're busy adulting and all that."

I grinned. "Tell them hello for me. And I promise, drinks on me when I get this job."

"I'll hold you to that! Catch you later."

I ended the call, then resumed my research, barely skimming over the company history before a sudden yawn confirmed that sleep was on the way. The time on my phone also told me it was time to get ready for bed if I wanted to be fresh and alert tomorrow. A quick shower, and I slipped under the covers. For some reason, the sleepiness had made a U-turn, and I was now wide awake. I stared at the blank ceiling above me, reflecting on my mom's last boss and how badly things had gone down. Total embarrassment. My cheeks grew hot as the memory of that night in the hotel assailed me. No matter how often I tried to keep the embarrassment at bay, it came back stronger than before each time I thought about it.

I still remembered the piercing grey eyes of the stranger, lashing me with judgement and anger. They'd haunted me for five years, making me want to curl into my skin. The weirdest thing was, although he made me feel like absolute shit that night, I remembered how attractive he was. I'd never imagined a man being beautiful until that night. Chiseled features, his torso sculpted to perfection with the beads of water trailing down his body, disappearing into the towel that covered his lower half. Heat filled my body when I recalled his thick erection pressing against the fabric. I squirmed in bed, a sudden ache between my thighs.

It amazed me that even after five years, I still thought about him. Granted, he was a hard man to forget. It wasn't just his physical beauty. It was the power behind that gorgeous frame, the way he exuded confidence with every step, how he made me terrified, angry and horny all at once, without even trying. I turned on my side, pulling the covers over my head. After five years and a single encounter, I shouldn't be feeling this way. I shouldn't be thinking about him at all.

A part of me felt gratitude for meeting him that night. It made me reflect on my actions, and it forced me to change for good. On the other hand, I was glad this was such a huge city. I'd die of embarrassment if I ran into him again.

Chapter 3

Alyssa

"Honey, we should get going," my mom called from my door, fully dressed in her work clothes, hair pinned to the top of her head with her bright red lipstick carving her small mouth.

I glanced in the mirror one last time, loving how classy the outfit made me look. Pencil skirt, silky long-sleeved top and heels with my hair pinned similarly to my Mom's – a few loose tendrils hanging around my face.

"What do you think?" I asked her.

She walked toward me slowly, a smile on her face as her green eyes glistened. "You look amazing, sweetheart." She ran her hands down my arms. "Your dad would be proud."

I swallowed the lump that immediately formed in my throat and managed a smile. "We should go."

She nodded as I picked up my purse and left my room. Even though I had my own car, we decided to carpool today. Luckily for me, Mom had been working with Stag Technologies for twenty years, so she spent the entire car ride telling me everything I needed to know.

Still, I couldn't help the churning in my gut when we pulled into the parking lot. I took a deep breath, smoothing out my skirt, my palms getting sweatier by the minute.

Mom gave me a knowing smile and pulled me into a hug. "No need to be nervous, honey. Lorraine will take great care of you. If it makes you feel any better, I'll walk you to the interview room."

I nodded. "Thanks, Mom."

We walked to the elevator, my heart dancing in my chest. There was no reason to be so nervous. I'd known Lorraine for most of my life. Still, the unease followed me all the way to the executive floor where we got off, then walked down a long hallway, the clicking of our heels echoing in my ear.

We walked past huge double doors with gold-plated handles. The CEO's office. I remembered the times Tony snuck me inside, the afternoon spent making out on his desk. I shook the memories from my head and kept moving. The walk seemed endless, but soon, we were just inches away from the conference door.

"Good luck," Mom said with a reassuring smile, and I knocked on the wooden door.

Well, here goes nothing.

The interview—well, it was more than a catching-up conversation—took twenty minutes, after which Lorraine announced that the job was mine, but I'd need to meet the CEO first. My heart raced as she led me back the way Mom and I had come, stopping in front of the doors with the gold handles. She pressed a card against the keypad and, after a beep, pulled the door open. Another short walk down the hallway, past a desk I suspected was my workstation, pausing in front of another glass door, currently frosted, a feature I knew all too well.

Lorraine knocked and waited for the answer.

"Come," the deep voice echoed, and I almost jumped out of my skin. I didn't know why I was still so nervous since the interview was already finished, but my heart rate spiked, the pulse beating in my ears.

Lorraine pushed the door open and entered. I followed behind, stepping inside, the scent of rosewood hitting my nostrils at once. My new boss stood at the glass window that overlooked the busy city, his broad back turned to us, one hand tucked in his pockets. His silver hair was neatly groomed, perfectly coiffed on top, faded at the sides and back. A charcoal-grey suit covered his athletic body, expensive-looking, tailored to perfection.

Lorraine cleared her throat. "Mr. Madden, this is Alyssa Reynolds, your new assistant."

The smiling, confident woman I spoke to a few minutes ago had disappeared. Beside me was her rigid shell, a slight tremor in her voice.

My breath paused as Mr. Madden slowly turned, and my heart thrummed even faster as our gazes locked. I blinked once to see if I was imagining things, but his face had been engraved in my mind for such a long time; there was no way I'd forget.

My vision blurred as I stared at him, white-hot embarrassment pooling inside me as I remembered that awful night. A soft splat pulled me from my shock. My folder had fallen to the floor.

I blinked again to clear the fog from my eyes, my cheeks running hot as I reached down.

"So sorry, Mr. Madden," Lorraine said with a nervous chuckle. "It's her first day. She's a little overwhelmed."

"Leave us, Mrs. Cambridge."

Lorraine managed a tight smile at the gruff order, gave me a look that said, *'Good luck, you'll need it!'* and then all but ran from the office. My gaze followed her as she left, the soft click of the door sounding more like a drumbeat. It immediately sunk in that I was now alone with the man who had haunted my dreams for five years. The embarrassing moment I thought was dead and buried safely in my head now fought its way to the surface, filling me with dread. I was afraid to look up at him. All I wanted to do was run through the door Lorraine had just left through, but for some reason, my feet remained grounded to the floor — almost frozen as I stood there.

There was a soft swish as he moved, and I braced myself. This was it, the moment he'd fire me from the job before I even began. Shortest employment in history.

A long beat passed, and nothing. No more movement, no talking. I dared to glance up and saw he had already moved to his chair, looking straight at me with no sign of emotion on his chiseled face. Perhaps he didn't remember me? Was that the case?

With a swift movement of his hand, he directed me to sit without saying a word. I looked at the empty chair in front of him and weighed my options. Not that I had much. Stiffly, I moved to the chair and took a seat, trying to settle my galloping heart.

He took a seat across from me and leaned back in his chair, his grey eyes just as cold as the last time I remembered. He had a low stubble that was mostly grey, covering his stern jawline and his full lips.

I swallowed hard as we made eye contact. His expression remained unreadable. There was no hint of recognition in his eyes, which soon made me relax. Mr. Madden didn't remember me.

I cleared my throat, the silence in the room forcing me to say something. "Nice to meet you, Mr. Madden. I'm really grateful for the opportunity to work with you."

A ghost of a smile played at his lips – one I might have missed if my eyes weren't glued to his face.

"We've met before, haven't we, Ms. Reynolds? I clearly remember you curled up in my bed five years ago."

Embarrassment immediately coursed through me, heating my face, forcing my gaze to the floor. *Just open up and swallow me already. Please.*

Chapter 4

Jax

I must be fucking cursed.

Yes, there was no other explanation. Not only did I inherit a company that had more trouble under the surface than I'd been aware of, not only was my mother riding my ass for a daughter-in-law and grandkids, but my temporary assistant turned out to be the last person I expected—the last woman I wanted to see walking through those doors.

When my HR director informed me that my new assistant would be hired this morning, I imagined a meek little lamb with oversized glasses and a nervous countenance, someone like Marjorie, my old assistant who was now off on maternity leave. When she told me it was our senior manager's daughter, someone only a year out of college, I almost said no. I didn't want a little girl trying to do the job; I wanted someone with experience.

Mrs. Reynold's flawless track record at this company battled with my reluctance. She was an invaluable asset to the business. I didn't want to lose her because I refused to give her daughter a chance.

So I said yes. Never in my wildest dreams – and trust, they were wild – did I imagine this being the outcome. Imagine my shock when I turned and found *her* standing there. The girl from five years ago who'd been in my hotel room, only she was no girl now; she was a woman, a stunning one. Back then, she was a pretty little thing, that neat, petite body now transformed into a beautiful figure that made me brace for many sleepless nights ahead.

Alyssa Reynolds was her name.

And she had no idea how many times she'd plagued my thoughts over the years. A face I would be crazy to forget — one I *couldn't* forget even if I tried, and trust me, I've tried like hell. Few men would want to fantasize about a woman who'd slipped into their hotel bed naked, waiting for another man.

I didn't think I would see her again, especially after she ran from my hotel room in a fit of sobs, no doubt embarrassed over the mix-up. But here she was in living color, pale-faced, staring at me wide-eyed. She remembered who I was, and it terrified the shit out of her. I didn't blame her. On a good day, I could be quite intimidating. Add our uncomfortable encounter and the fact I was now her boss... it surprised me she was still standing there. I'd expected a quick dash out the door the second she realized who I was.

Something told me she wasn't the meek person staring back at me right now. Instead, there was something bold under the surface. Her little attempt to seduce my colleague was a telltale sign.

"Nice to meet you, Mr. Madden," she said, her voice slightly shaky, but she still tried to keep up a smile.

I clenched my jaw as I held back mine. Was she really going to pretend like four years ago didn't happen?

"We've met before, haven't we, Ms. Reynolds? I clearly remember you curled up in my bed five years ago," I said, watching as she paled right in front of me.

Her mouth opened and closed again. She cleared her throat. "Um... yeah," her gaze shifted to her lap, where she picked at her nails. "Yes, Sir, we've met." She looked up at me again, her hazel eyes holding me in place. "Not my finest moment, but it doesn't define who I am today, I assure you."

I'll be the judge of that. I gave a curt nod, gestured to her folder and stretched out my hand. She frowned, staring down at my hand.

"Give me the folder," I emphasized, wiggling my fingers impatiently.

Her frown disappeared, and she quickly scooped up the folder and handed it to me.

I looked over the resume, trying my best to concentrate on the details, but it was a struggle. Very unlike me. Very rarely did a woman scatter my thoughts, and Ms. Reynolds had done it twice now. I became aware of everything; her nervous shifting in the seat, the clicking of her fingernails as she flicked them, the scent of her perfume...

I shook my head and looked over her documents, realizing Ms. Reynolds wasn't just a beautiful face. Even if I wanted to reject her, it would be a stupid decision. She was a smart girl, a potential asset to my company.

Yet...

I'd lived on the straight and narrow for my entire adult life, avoiding potential disasters so skillfully one could call me lucky. But it wasn't luck. It was the effect of making careful decisions. Hiring Ms. Reynolds wasn't one of them.

For five years, she crossed my mind. One encounter and she left an impression on me, one I couldn't shake off. Imagine having her so close, always at my beck and call. It spelled nothing but trouble. Alyssa Reynolds was a distraction I didn't need.

"No working experience?" I asked, my voice much cooler than I intended.

Her shoulders stiffened with the same tension that filled her face. "Um – well... I worked at a non-profit after leaving college, Mr. Madden. It's right there—"

"Let me rephrase. Have you ever been gainfully employed?"

Her mouth opened up before the answer came. "I'm afraid not. If you don't mind me asking, Sir, is this an interview? Because I already had one with Mrs. Cambridge."

I raised a questioning brow at her, and she deflated in her seat. "I'm conducting my own assessment, Ms. Reynolds, to confirm if you're a great fit."

She nodded. "I'm sorry for interrupting."

"Hmm," I lowered my gaze back to the papers. "How well do you work under pressure?"

"I– I would say pretty efficiently. College was pretty hectic, but I worked my way around the stress."

"This isn't college," I replied sharply.

"I'm well aware... Sir." There was an edge to her voice that surprised me.

I closed the folder and eased back in my chair as I assessed her. She was beautiful – no, stunning, and I couldn't help staring, wishing her hair wasn't pinned at the top of her head like some middle-aged woman. I wanted it loose and dangling down her cleavage like she wore it four years ago. I wanted –

I stopped, wanting to scold myself for the filthy thoughts that surfaced. This was work, a professional space. There was no place for the things I wanted to do with her.

None whatsoever.

But I ignored the warning in my head, closing the folder with a snap. "The job is yours, Ms. Cambridge," I announced, and her hazel eyes widened.

"What?"

"You start tomorrow at eight."

Her small forehead wrinkled as she stared at me as if she expected me to change my mind. Realizing I had nothing else to say, she nodded and swallowed, reaching for her folder.

I handed it to her, and our fingers brushed against each other. She stiffened for a fleeting second before collecting herself and muttering, "Thank you."

There was some hesitance before she smoothed her skirt and moved toward the door. Though my commonsense warned me not to, I found it hard to look away, taking in the gentle flare of her hips and the bouncing of her ass as she walked out.

Regret filled me as the door closed behind her. This would lead to nothing good. Workplace policy aside, I couldn't date a woman like Ms. Reynolds. I hadn't forgotten how she'd slipped into my hotel room to seduce a man about to be married. She was a younger woman back then, but it still spoke volumes about her character. I didn't care how innocent she appeared; my instincts told me she was nothing but trouble. I couldn't handle another complication on my plate right now.

My cell phone rang. I glanced at the screen with a groan. Speaking of complication...

I breathed a deep sigh, pressing the phone to my ear. "Hi, Mom."

"Hello, my lovebug," Mom crooned, and I imagined the wide smile on her face. "How are you doing? I haven't heard from you in a while now."

I resisted the urge to roll my eyes. "Mom, we spoke yesterday morning."

"Oh, we did, didn't we?" she replied with a laugh. "Oh, the days are going by so fast."

"Can I help you with something? I'm at work."

"When are you coming by for a visit? I miss you."

I glanced at the calendar on my desk. "On the month's end, maybe."

"Great! Because I'm having the Van Der Beeks over for dinner next Saturday night. Remember their daughter Sarah?"

Of course, I remembered the cute blonde Mom made me invite to the prom when I was seventeen. "Yes, I do."

"Well, she's back from her modeling tour in Europe, and she'll be at dinner, too. Maybe you can rekindle your little romance..." Her voice trailed off, and I didn't miss the hopelessness in her tone.

"We were just friends, Mom. Absolutely no romance," I corrected.

"And all that can change come Friday night. Think of how lovely it would be if you got together. Think of the beautiful kids you could have."

"Mom..." My warning tone came low and hard.

"What? Jax, I'm sixty-eight years old. I'm the only person in my bridge club without grandkids. Don't you think it's time to put me out of my misery?"

I threw my head back with a groan. My mom's request for grandkids had been a source of contention for ten years, around the same time she pushed me to get married. Back then, I'd been busy building my empire. There was no time for anything but casual dating—definitely no space for kids.

Now that I'd achieved most of my goals, I often entertained the thought of settling down, but deep down, I wasn't ready. Not until I settled an important score.

When the time was right, I'd meet my soulmate, have the fancy wedding and the cute babies. Whatever Mom wanted. Except Sarah. I'd never marry that superficial brat if someone paid me.

I ended the call after promising Mom I'd be home at the end of the month, then I poured myself into work. It took an entire hour to settle down and focus on the list of tasks in front of me. Ms. Reynolds, with her beautiful face and curvy body, was a huge distraction, again making me wonder if I'd made the biggest mistake of my life.

Chapter 5

Alyssa

I STILL COULDN'T BELIEVE it. The stranger from that hotel room, the main character in my dreams for five years, was my mother's boss. Such a strange coincidence! I lay in bed, not knowing whether to laugh or cry. I should have turned the job down. I should have told Jax Madden thanks for the offer, but no thanks and walked out that door. Being in his presence intimidated the shit out of me, and I'd only spent half an hour in his office. How the hell would I survive three months sharing the same space as him?

I was still shocked that he'd even offered me the job, especially after that comment about my work experience. Did he have an ulterior motive? Did he get off on seeing me burn with shame whenever I remembered that awful night?

Or maybe...

I sat up in bed as a thought occurred.

Did he hire me because he wanted to score? Did he assume I was still that stupid slut who'd just open my legs for any man?

No. I didn't think so. From what Mom told me, Mr. Madden had written the company policy banning office romance. There was no way he'd go to such lengths only to break his own rule.

I relaxed with a deep sigh, more confused than ever. Whatever his motives were, I'd tread carefully. It took half an hour on Google to learn how powerful Jax Madden was. He invented his first video game at twenty years old, and by twenty-five, he was the town's youngest multi-millionaire. He'd acquired and sold more tech companies than any other mogul in the county. By age thirty, he'd become a multi-billionaire when he sold his prototype to an overseas conglomerate.

Again, Mom was right. Jax Madden could open the right doors if I played my cards right, which meant showing up for work on time, keeping my head down and doing the work he paid me to do.

"Damn, if I didn't stop by and talk to your mom downstairs, I'd think the interview was shit."

I eased up from my bed to find Liz moving through my open door, concern on her face. "Are you okay?"

I sighed. "I'm fine, I guess. Only you knew the full story."

"Well, tell me what's going on. That's what I'm here for anyway," she said, easing her hand from behind her back and revealing a bottle of red wine.

I sat up in bed. "What are we celebrating?"

"Your new job, of course! It's a huge deal that you scored a gig on your first week back home."

I scoffed as I shimmied to the edge, Liz sitting beside me. "It's not that serious, and after what I have to tell you, you'll think twice about celebrating."

"Well, dang, don't hold me in suspense any longer."

"Remember five years ago when I snuck into Tony Bancroft's hotel room?"

Liz shook her head, scoffing. "You've had some wild moments back in the day, but that was crazy. How could I forget? Such a pity you forgot to get Mr. Mystery's name and number, though. He definitely sounded like your type."

I rolled my eyes. "Well... I have his name now."

"For sure? How come?"

"Take a wild guess."

It took her a second, but then her eyes widened, her mouth falling open. "No way!"

"Yep, the man who'd made me feel like shit for weeks is actually Jax Madden, my new boss."

"What the fuck!" she blurted.

"Imagine walking in and seeing him standing there? I don't know why I didn't faint. It was definitely a moment to sink through the floor," I replied with a groan.

"Damn, that's – how did you even get the job? If I remember clearly, you said he was an asshole to you."

"He was, and I have a feeling he still is. I think he hired me to make my life a living hell for some reason."

"But why, though?" Liz asked. "You did nothing to him."

"I don't know... but he seemed angry that night. I don't know why. Maybe Tony married his sister or something," I assumed with a shrug.

Liz sighed. "Oh, Lord ... I don't even know what to say. This is weird. *That* must have been weird for you."

"Oh, believe me, it was the worst."

"Why didn't you just say no?"

I raked my hands through my hair. "Maybe I would've, but in the moment, I couldn't even think straight. I'm glad I didn't, though."

"Why not?" she asked, raising a brow.

"Because he's well-connected. You said it, Liz. Working with Jax Madden could catapult my career."

"Yes, I did, back when I thought he was a grumpy old man. Would you want to work with someone who intimidates you like that?"

I shrugged. "I mean, it's work, and if he's professional about it, I don't see a huge problem. Besides, my workspace stands outside his office. I won't see him every second of the day."

Liz shrugged, shifting on the bed. "Well, if you're comfortable..."

I wasn't. It terrified me when I thought of my first day on the job. Liz didn't need to know that, though. In fact, it would be my little secret. "I'll be fine, Liz, don't worry about me."

"Okay, now that this face has a name, I can't wait to see it." She pulled her phone from her pocket and quickly typed in it. "Goddamn... Now he's the definition of a silver fox! The man is fine, Ally!" she gushed, her mouth hanging open as she stared at me.

"Yeah, he's alright," I replied casually, hoping the lie did not read on my face.

She laughed. "You know he's hot. I'm not into older guys, but this one," she paused and moaned wistfully. "This one, I'd definitely climb like a tree."

I scoffed in response, ignoring the flutter in my stomach and the sudden image of me straddling Jax Madden on his office chair.

"Oh, wow, he's almost as rich as my dad," Liz commented as she scrolled on. "No wife or kids... just a string of model-like girls he's dated in the past — no surprise there."

I pretended to seem uninterested, but my mind processed everything Liz had to say. I wanted to know everything about this mystery man who'd made another shocking appearance in my life.

"Yeah, sounds like the typical old rich guy," I murmured.

Liz snorted. "Well, old isn't exactly the word I'd use. He's just forty-two, and he looks better than most guys our age."

I pulled in a breath, getting off the bed. "Anyway, no point in letting this wine go to waste. Let's have at it."

"Change the subject all you want, Ally. We both know you're attracted to him. He's your type." She got up, looking me up and down with a smirk. "Oh, I forgot; you're a good girl now. There will be no seducing Jax Madden at the office, right?"

"That's right," I replied, leading the way downstairs.

"Mmh-Mhm," she said behind me. "Once a bad girl, always a bed girl. It just takes the right guy—or wrong—however you look at it, to unearth that dark side. Something tells me he could be the one."

I shook my head. "Not a chance, Liz. You should've seen the way he looked at me. He's not interested in me. And even if he was," I said with a raised voice, interrupting whatever she was about to say. "It's against the rules to date an employee. He would never touch me with a ten-foot pole."

"Never say never," Liz replied, waving her index finger. "You would be amazed to find out Jax is a rule breaker, just like you."

"*Was* a rule breaker," I corrected.

"Whatever. We're going to have this conversation again, and I'll say I told you so."

Not on my life, I thought.

I DIDN'T KNOW WHY PICKING out my outfit today seemed harder than before, but I spent two hours deciding on what to wear before settling on a burgundy dress that was a little too snug, but after wasting so much time digging in my closet, I was almost late for work. No time to choose something else.

I quickly showered and did the same professional, 'corporate' hairstyle before I fetched my bag and left the room. Since mom had already left, I drove my own car. But I didn't mind, considering I needed the time to clear my head without my mom's chatter.

Well on my way, I wondered what my first day would be like. If it went south, if Mr. Madden scared me even more than he did yesterday, then I'd have no choice but to quit. I refused to suffer in a job that made me uncomfortable. Jax Madden seemed like the kind of workaholic boss who would push his staff to bust their ass, too, and while that wouldn't be a bad thing, our brief history made me wonder if he would push me more than the others. His coldness toward me made me wonder; did I do something wrong that I wasn't aware of?

Once I parked in the huge parking lot, I rechecked my makeup and hurried upstairs, releasing a soft sigh when the elevator door opened on the executive floor.

Here goes nothing. Jax Madden, let's see what you've got for me. Hopefully, you're not as demanding as Mom makes you out to be.

The workday had just begun, but people were already at their desks, eyes locked on computer screens, fingers busy typing away. I hurried to my workstation and put down my bag, immediately noticing a note taped to the front of the monitor.

Come to my office.

I didn't need to guess the source of this neatly written command. With a deep breath, I made my way to my boss' office, pausing for a second at his door before I knocked. The firm "Come," made me uneasy, but I pushed the door open, my eyes immediately landing on his desk, his head buried in a folder. My heart fluttered when he looked up, his reading glasses on, which made him even more attractive. As if sensing my thoughts, he took them off, placed them on his desk and leaned back in his chair, his gaze unwavering as he gave me a thorough once-over.

"Good morning, Sir."

"Good morning, Ms. Reynolds," he said. "You're late."

I quickly glanced at my watch, frowning as I looked back at him. "I'm actually right on time, Sir."

"Being right on time means you're late. You should already be at your desk, your computer on and the first task of the day already underway. See that we never have this conversation again. Understood?"

"Yes, Sir," I reply, swallowing my annoyance. I was literally standing at my desk by eight-thirty; what was his problem?

With his expression still firm, he pushed a document in front of me. "Your contract."

I stared at him blankly for a beat, then a flash of impatience ran across his face.

"Is there something wrong?" he asked.

"Not really—um—I just wondered what it is," I replied, pointing to the document.

His face relaxed a little. Just a little. There was still a slight hardness there. "These are the terms and conditions of your employment. Once you sign, it means you agree to abide by the rules of the company. To break them means exposing yourself to a potential lawsuit. I had HR send it down, so I could assess the details myself."

"L—lawsuit?" I stammered, the rest of his response hazy.

"Nothing to worry about once you stick to the rules. Only the rebellious would be worried."

I recognized the slight jab at me, but I pretended not to notice. Of course, there was a contract, which meant it wouldn't be so easy to quit if things went south like I'd imagined.

I glanced down at the document before looking back at him, my gut tightening. "I'm not worried at all."

"Good. I thought as much."

I approached his desk and took a seat as I reached for the contract, a pen beside it. I took both and read the contents, doing my very best to concentrate with his eyes on me. Apparently, this position could be extended after three months if there were no issues.

Hmm. We'll see if that works out.

The pen lingered for a beat over the slot for my signature; then I quickly scribbled my name across the blank line. It seemed I'd just sealed my fate to three months of torment, but as I glanced at Mr. Madden's calm expression, it made me relax a little. Maybe I was overthinking things. Maybe he wouldn't be hard on me.

"All done." I smiled and pushed back the contract toward him.

He checked my signature, then nodded. "Your desktop is already set up with my schedule for today. Mrs. Cambridge will brief you on what is required of you."

"Okay."

I got up to leave, then paused when he cleared his throat. "And Ms. Reynolds..." I held my breath. "I'm sure you read the details of the contract, but let me emphasize. I don't condone fraternization in the workplace."

"Understood, Sir," I replied, pushing my chair back and quickly leaving the room, hurrying to my desk where I replayed what he said. Of all the rules, why did he stress that one? Did he think I had aspirations of becoming the office slut?

Sure, he had reasons to think little of me after what happened that night. If only he knew the truth, that I didn't know Tony had another woman in his life. I wasn't a home wrecker, just a girl who tried to mask her pain by doing dumb shit. I wasn't that girl anymore. I'd worked my butt off to prove how much I'd changed.

I turned on the computer, using the instructions taped to the desk to log on and access my daily schedule. The first two-hour slot was an orientation session with HR, a session I was already half an hour late for.

Taking a pen and notepad from the drawer, I made my way to the HR department, passing Mr. Madden's office as I went. A part of me wanted to change his perception of me. For some reason, it bothered me. I wanted to get on his good side and stay there. The problem was, I didn't know how.

Chapter 6

Jax

I wished she wasn't so attractive. Those long legs, gorgeous body, sweet smile... if only those weren't components of her that really got my blood flowing. If only her presence didn't trigger a response in my body, an ache I'd never experienced in my life. It was hard to look at Alyssa Reynolds and not itch to touch her. Fuck that. I wanted to do more than touch.

I'd wanted to do more than touch her since the night I found her in my bed. For five years, I imagined the feel of those rose-pink nipples in my mouth, that curvy body writhing beneath me as I pleasured her, the soft moans from her thick lips as she came apart for me. Five years, and I became content with the memory of the woman who made me feel alive. Intrigued. I never thought I'd see her again.

Now she was here in my space, and there was nothing I could do about it. Not only did I learn there was a significant age gap between us, much more than I thought—she was an eighteen-year-old when I met her for fuck's sake, not twenty years old like she claimed—there was the workplace policy to consider. A policy I enforced—the irony—but one that was totally necessary at the time.

Tony had been my colleague for years, and I respected him, but he almost ran the company to the ground with the loose culture he had going on. Sexual harassment lawsuits hit the company left, right and center, making a huge dent in the bottom line. Getting that rule in place seemed a great idea at the time, but now it had come back to bite me in the ass.

Or maybe not. Rule or no rule, I should leave Ms. Reynolds alone. I'd grown tired of casual relationships. I wanted a woman, not a plaything. Definitely not someone half my age.

Three months, and she would be out of my space. I couldn't wait.

Marking the date in my mental calendar, I buried myself in work for a few hours until Ms. Reynolds knocked on my door to announce the client for my twelve o'clock meeting had arrived. She stepped aside to let him in, then hurried away, and I tried not to watch her ass as she went. Tried, but failed. Epic fail.

"Mr. Palmer, I'm glad you could make it," I said, addressing the middle-aged client. When I got his email about a business productivity software that could boost the company's profits, I cleared my schedule to meet with him.

"Thank you for having me. To be honest, I'm surprised you took this meeting, considering how long I've been trying to get through to you."

"Well, I've just been made aware of your product, and there are rumors it could do wonders for Stag's recovery," I replied. "So, here we are. Let's do business."

There was a sudden knock on the door, and at my response, Ms. Reynolds appeared with a tray of teacups, sandwiches, hot water and ingredients for tea. The smile on her face seemed forced, but she kept it in place until she left the room. I noticed Mr. Palmer's eyes watching her and gave him a pointed stare when our eyes met. He shrugged, his face going red.

"As we were," I prompted.

"Right. I'm really looking forward to a partnership with Stag Technologies.

I scoffed. "This is not a partnership, Mr. Palmer. I want to buy your patent. Name your price."

He shifted in his chair, the smile faltering from his face. "My patent isn't for sale. I was hoping to contribute toward lifting your dying company, but that's obviously not what you want."

I clenched my teeth. "Stag Technologies isn't dying. Get your facts straight."

He smirked. "Come on, Madden. Word on the street was that the company was already half-dead before you took over, and from what I've heard, you've done little to change that since you got here. You've been injecting your money to keep things afloat, haven't you?"

A scowl formed on my face. "What's your point. Mr. Palmer?"

"You're a wealthy man, Mr. Madden, but your funds aren't unlimited. You should probably change your tactic before this company turns you back into the pauper you've worked so hard to escape."

My fingers tightened around my pen at his mention of my past. "Are you done?"

He seemed taken aback by my cool response, sighing heavily as he rose from his seat. "Maybe you'll want to give my suggestion some thought."

"It's a no, Palmer."

He strained a laugh. "Ok, well then, suit yourself. Can't say I didn't try."

I gave him a hard glare as I sat there with my teeth tightly clenched. "See yourself out."

Palmer nodded curtly, his slender shoulders swinging as he left my office. When the door clicked shut, I reached for the office phone.

"I'd like a copy of the latest financial reports, please," I told my CFO on the other end. Then, without awaiting his response, I ended the call and raked my fingers through my hair.

With a team of twenty-five hundred staff members and eight branches nationwide, it wasn't easy keeping track of every single detail. I knew the company's bottom line was a mess, and I'd been doing everything in my power to change it, but after a year, there'd been no improvement. It was still early days, so I didn't judge myself too harshly, but something had to give. I wanted a turn of the tide real soon.

A partnership was out of the question. So was a merger. I wanted to take Stag Technologies back to the top on my own. It was the only way to achieve my endgame.

A soft knock came at the door, and I mentally cursed, hating the disturbance since I hardly had any time to collect myself.

"Come," I snapped, harsher than I intended.

The door slowly opened, and Ms. Reynolds stepped through the small crack she allowed herself. My temper immediately calmed. I straightened in the seat, giving her my full attention.

"Sorry to disturb you, Mr. Madden, but I'm about to take lunch," she said.

It took me a second to realize what she had said. Though my gaze was on her lips, her words were the farthest thing from my mind. When I finally processed, I nodded firmly and watched as she disappeared again.

The CFO emailed the draft of this quarter's financial reports, and I spent the next half hour running through our expenses, then set a reminder to have Ms. Reynolds book a meeting with each department manager. First order of business; reduce department costs.

The hint of an incoming headache made me leave the office for some much-needed fresh air, which meant walking across the street to my favorite café that served the best coffee in the city. I stepped through the front door, immediately seeing Ms. Reynolds with her mother having lunch at the far back. She seemed animated, wearing a genuine smile. There was no tension, no fear. She seemed relaxed, a stark contrast to her demeanor around me.

Usually, I didn't care what my staff thought of me or whether they feared me. In fact, I encouraged that response from them. Being nice and friendly only got you fucked when people walked over you. I'd learned that the hard way. I took great pleasure in seeing them scramble to keep things in order when I came around. The fear in their eyes was like a drug. With Ms. Reynolds, it was quite the opposite. I didn't want her to fear me. I wanted to see pleasure in her eyes when she looked at me.

There was only one way to fix that, but it wasn't an option. I couldn't befriend her. Not only was it inappropriate, but dangerous. Even with that cute smile and innocent-looking face, Ms. Reynolds had the power to weaken me. I sensed it. As much as it bothered me, there was nothing I could do about her fear.

After placing my order with the cashier, I glanced back over, watching as she rubbed her nape, throwing her head back and closing her eyes, the action triggering my filthiest thought. How would she react as my cock filled her? Would her eyes close in ecstasy? Would she moan my name? Would her fingers grip my skin like they gripped the back of her neck just now?

"Your coffee, Sir."

I returned my gaze to the woman in front of me, who handed me my coffee, her fingers deliberately brushing mine. Her flirty smile did nothing for me, but I gave her a responding smile and took the cup, giving Ms. Reynolds another quick glance before leaving the café.

Again, I wondered if I'd made the right decision in hiring her. It was one thing to fantasize about her, thinking I'd never see her again, but it was an entirely different ball game with her now working so close to me. I considered myself a disciplined man, but for the first time in my life, I had doubts about my self-control. I didn't understand why, considering I'd dated more beautiful women than Ms. Reynolds, and they'd never triggered this reaction in me. What was it about her that made me want to bend the rules? After all these years of being on the straight and narrow, would a twenty-three-year-old finally ruin my life?

Chapter 7

Alyssa

It had almost been a week since I'd been working at Stag Technologies, yet it felt like an entire month. It wasn't just Mr. Madden's demanding schedule that made the tenure seem longer than it was, although it contributed a great deal. My butt hardly hit the seat in the mornings when the phone rang, his deep, commanding voice springing me into action, after which I'd spend the entire day running back and forth, fulfilling his every wish.

The physical labor was a lot, but it didn't compare to the emotional load that took a toll on my body. Being attracted to a man who scared me, wanting to rip my clothes off for him, yet having the urge to hide under my desk whenever he stormed by, his office door slamming behind him, well, it was a mind fuck, to say the least. I didn't understand why he affected me like this, why there was such a clash of my feelings for him.

Did it matter, though? The man was my boss – my mother's boss and the chances of him even looking at me were as rare as a blue moon. Mr. Madden created the 'no romance' company policy. I doubted he'd break his own rule.

I saved a file I'd been working on, then powered down the computer, smiling to myself. The old Alyssa would face this challenge head-on, pushing him to commit the ultimate sin.

One taste and he'd be hooked, kicking that stupid rule to the curb—

No. It wasn't stupid. Rules were made to keep the shit-show from happening. Like the ones that I'd broken as a teenager. Look where they'd brought me. Thank God Mr. Madden had a moral compass. What if I had sneaked into a sexual predator's room instead? I shuddered as I imagined the outcome, happy I returned home alive and well.

Footsteps approached my desk as I opened the bottom drawer to retrieve my bag. I looked up, my jaw slackening when I saw the familiar face.

"Blake? What are you doing here?"

The guy I met a week ago at the bar gave me a smile fit for any toothpaste commercial, his hands bracing the edge of my desk. "Wow, I'm shocked you remember my name," he replied.

"How could I forget? I loved that dress, and you came pretty close to ruining it."

He straightened, the smile fading. "Again, I'm sorry about that."

I waved him off. "It's fine. What are you doing here?"

He jerked his thumb toward the HR department. "I came for an interview, and I'm starting Monday."

I raised my brow. "Woah, that's awesome. Congrats."

He smiled. "Are you related to anyone working here? There was a manager in the interview who looked just like you."

"That sounds like my mom. Mrs. Reynolds, right?"

He nodded. "Yep. She's going to be my new boss. Well, after I speak to the bigger boss for a few minutes." He cocked his head at Madden's office. "Heard he's scary as hell."

"Just keep eye contact. Don't let him see you squirm, and you'll be fine."

"Eye contact, no squirming. Got it."

"Good look. And good seeing you, Blake."

He nodded. "You too..." there was a short pause. "Maybe sometime we could er– grab lunch or something. Catch up on old times," he said with a chuckle.

I chuckled back. "Old times, my ass. I only met you once."

"Yet, it feels like I've known you forever."

"Corny."

"Or romantic. Depends on how you look at it. So..." He leaned forward with his hands resting on top of the desk. "Are we on for lunch?"

"Kinley."

Jax Madden's deep voice sent my reply flying down my throat. Blake paled, his eyes widening at me. He swallowed visibly as he turned to Mr. Madden standing at the door, lashing Blake with a hard stare. I was so caught up talking to Blake I didn't notice when he stepped out.

"Mr. Madden," Blake said, a slight tremor in his voice. "I—I'm—"

"Late." The single word came out cold as ice, even colder than his expression. "I don't take kindly to people making me wait. This is your first and only strike. Let's go."

I watched as Blake hurried into the office, Mr. Madden sending me a cool stare before he closed the door behind them.

Without wasting a second, I grabbed my bag, in a hurry to get out of there. From the look on my boss' face, I had a feeling there was a strike against me, too.

Only I didn't know why.

"HOW ABOUT HIM?" LIZ asked, pointing to a dark-haired guy who just walked past the bar.

I took him in for a second. He was attractive, dressed casually in a T-shirt and ripped jeans. He brushed a lock of hair from his face, which earned him another point. "He's alright," I replied.

"Alright?" Liz exclaimed. "That there is a nine, my friend. What's wrong with you?"

"He's not my type," I replied with a shrug.

"Oh, I forgot. He's not twice your age."

I nudged her side, and she giggled, then waved to the bartender to refill our order. This was just what I needed after such a tense week. Relaxing at the bar, sipping my favorite cocktail, my Uber driver on standby...

Two more days and back to the reality of that pressure cooker with Mr. Madden. I didn't want to think about that, though. Not right now.

"When was the last time you even had sex?" Liz asked as the bartender placed our drinks before us. He smirked, obviously overhearing her question. My cheeks heated as I glared at her.

"What?" she asked innocently.

"Why don't you repeat that question? Only this time, shout so the entire bar hears you."

"It's called fucking. Everyone does it," she replied, rolling her eyes. "I don't recall you being this stuck up." She shook my shoulder. "Loosen up a little."

I twirled my olives into my martini and pulled in a breath. "Fine. But there's nothing to talk about."

"Did you really spend five years in D.C. without getting laid? I don't believe that for a second."

"Believe what you want. Doesn't make it less true."

"How come, though? Does this have anything to do with that hotel room disaster?"

I groaned. "OMG. Can we not talk about that? There's not a day that goes by where I don't regret making a fool of myself."

"Did that night kill your sexual vibe or something? You did a complete one-eighty afterward. No partying, no messing around... you were like a ghost."

I pulled in a breath. "I don't know. For years, I convinced myself that the embarrassment turned me off from men. To be honest, that wasn't the case."

Liz cocked a brow. "Why do I feel like this is about to get juicy as hell?"

"It's not juicy. It's disastrous. I have a thing for my boss. Five years, and I didn't forget him for a day. I don't understand. I only met him—if you can call him that—for ten minutes. How can such a brief encounter affect me so much?"

"Holy shit." She stared at me with her red lips agape, her drink pausing midair. "This is definitely juicy. You want to fuck your boss!"

"Again, not loud enough," I replied sarcastically. "The people at the door didn't hear you."

She covered her mouth with a giggle. "Sorry. But there's nothing wrong with wanting him, Ally. He's totally hot, loaded, definitely your type. And with you working so close, it's the perfect opportunity to—"

"No. No, no, no."

"Come on, Ally. You made out with Tony Bancroft countless times in that office, and no one found out, and you didn't even work there then. There's no stopping you from getting what you want now."

"Are you insane? He's my boss, Liz."

"People fuck their bosses all the time, and if you're just looking for a fling, I don't see the problem."

My eyes widened. "You've clearly had too much to drink."

"And you haven't had enough," she threw back.

How about the company policy that forbids any office romance?"

"Did you miss the part where I said that no one needs to find out? You'll be gone in like three months. I don't see the problem with getting your hands dirty for a minute."

I sighed as I shook my head. "You're a terrible influence."

"That used to be your job, remember?"

I disregarded her last comment. "Even if I were bold enough to seduce Jax Madden, it wouldn't work. I think he hates me. The way he stares at me sometimes... it's scary."

Liz's eyes sparkled with mischief as she rocked on her seat. "Ooh... think of how intense the sex could be."

Imaginary butterflies filled my stomach. I bit my lips as my mind conjured the image of us fucking on his desk, my skirt hiked over my hips, his grip tight on my waist as he stroked me from behind. I squirmed on the seat, a slight chill leaving goosebumps on my skin.

"I've had too much to drink," I mumbled, resting my half-finished drink on the counter.

"You're actually considering this, aren't you?" Liz asked, the sparkle still in her eyes.

"No, I'm not," I replied firmly, almost biting my tongue with the lie. "I should be looking for a stable future. Not a fling."

"Are you really ready for marriage and kids? I don't believe that."

"Yes, eventually. This new me isn't a front, Liz. I want to fall in love, to be a mother, someone's wife. I want the suburban life. There's nothing wrong with that."

"I agree. But until then, until Mr. Right comes along, just enjoy living a little. If that includes fucking your boss, go right ahead."

I rolled my eyes. "I am not going to sleep with my boss."

"Think about it. You might spend the rest of your life wishing you did," she said, signaling to the bartender for another drink.

THAT NIGHT, I WENT to bed with Liz's 'advice' on my mind. She was right about being employed to Stag Industries for three months, and if my boss and I had a fling, it would end when my contract did, no harm done. That was the only sensible point she made, though. Jax Madden and I would never have an affair because he didn't have a thing for me. Better to tuck away my feelings for him and move on.

But the more I resisted my attraction to him, the more I yearned for him, and the more my stomach fluttered when I imagined his lips on me, his hands doing wonders to my body, giving me pleasure I'd never experienced in my life. I rolled onto my stomach, releasing a frustrated groan into the pillows. Of all the men I'd ever met, why was my attraction to him so strong?

Why Jax Madden?

Now more than ever, I regretted sneaking into his hotel room that night. If I hadn't, I wouldn't have been captivated by those intense grey eyes. I wouldn't have remembered every definition of those abs or seen the outline of his cock through that towel. The memory of his scent wouldn't have triggered the lingering urge to lose myself in him. I wouldn't be aching for him like this.

I sat up in bed, patting my damp forehead, wishing I didn't leave my stash of vibrators back in D.C. After an embarrassing incident in the airport last Christmas, I didn't dare pack them in my luggage when I moved back home. Just the memory of the customs officer examining my rose vibrator made me dump them all in the trash. I'd planned on buying new ones, anyway.

Now, I regretted not keeping one, at least. I needed to come. The sexual tension was too much to bear. Wiggling from my shorts, I spread my thighs, emitting a sigh when I touched myself. These fingers would do. At least, for tonight.

I tried not to think about him as I stroked the seam of my warm flesh, making my way to my hard clit. It was a useless attempt, though. I thought of nothing else but his tongue replacing my fingers, circling my clit, licking that sensitive spot below the hood, pushing me to an earth-shattering release that had me squirting all over the bedsheet. Sated, I dropped against the pillows, unable to stop myself from moaning his name.

But when I finally came down, my body still weak from my first climax in months, I realized one thing. Masturbation did nothing to quench my hunger for Jax Madden. In fact, my attraction to him was even stronger than before.

MONDAY MORNING, MR. Madden summoned me to his office the minute I got to my desk. Remembering the look he gave me last Friday, I grabbed my tablet and hurried to comply, pausing at the door to collect myself before I knocked. His one-word command brought me into his office in the next second — just the two of us.

He looked up from his computer, his gaze running over my figure for a brief second before returning to the screen. My heart fluttered in my chest as if trying to escape its cage. The silence lingered for a minute, each passing second leaving me tight with tension. My hands tapped against my thighs as I waited, the clicking of the keyboard the only sound in the room.

After a few minutes, I lost my patience. "Did you need anything, Sir?"

He gave me a look that clearly showed his displeasure at being interrupted. "Do you mind if I finish drafting this important email, Ms. Reynolds?"

"Not at all, Sir," I replied at once. *You could've waited until you were done before calling me to your office, though,* I wanted to add.

"Have a seat. I'm almost done," he said.

Suppressing a sigh, I sat in front of him, my eyes dropping to my lap. I didn't want to look at him. It was such a trigger, evoking thoughts that had no business in my head, especially in this professional space.

"Ms. Reynolds."

I didn't know how long I sat in that position, staring down at my hands, but it felt like some time had passed when I tentatively raised my head to meet Mr. Madden's inquisitive stare. "Sir?"

"Are you okay?"

The question caught me off guard, making me stutter. "Um—I—y-yes, Sir. I am."

"Are you sure? You seem quite..." His eyes searched my face. "Tense. One would think after such a weekend, you would be a little relaxed."

Such a weekend? "What do you mean by that?" I asked, puzzled. It was too farfetched to assume he'd followed me around all weekend. Even if he found me attractive, Jax Madden did not seem like the stalking type.

"You're what, twenty-three years old? I imagine you'd been out all weekend having fun."

"Oh." Why did I feel such disappointment that he hadn't been stalking me? "I had fun, I guess."

"Then why are you so tense?"

His questioning eyes locked with mine. I raised my shoulders in a slow shrug.

"Are you afraid of me, Alyssa?"

Hearing him say my name for the first time in that low, husky tone made me close my eyes, my entire body pulsing with an emotion foreign to me.

"I'm sorry," he said, regret now filling his voice. "That was highly inappropriate of me. I shouldn't have used your first name."

Highly inappropriate? Oh yes, my chances of getting laid by Jax Madden had just shot down to zero.

"I'm not afraid of you, Mr. Madden," I replied. "Well, not really. I..." My eyes dropped to my lap, and I flicked my fingernails, a habit when I grew nervous.

"Continue. This is a safe space," he assured me. "We have three months working together, and I need you comfortable."

"I can't help feeling like you hate me," I blurted, and his brows shot up. "Like you're piss—angry about that night."

His expression settled, a hint of amusement now on his face. "Ah, the elephant in the room. Why would I be angry?" he asked.

"I don't know. Maybe Tony—Mr. Bancroft's wife is your sister or something."

"I have no siblings."

"Oh."

"And even if she were, it would not justify hating you. You were a kid. Tony should've known better. Given his track record, I still don't expect much."

I nodded, still flicking my fingernails.

"Rest assured, Ms. Reynolds. I don't hate you. That notion couldn't be further from the truth."

Before I could ask what he meant by that, he reached into a drawer and pulled something out. "There's an important event on the weekend, and I need my assistant there with me." He slid a flyer on the table toward me.

I scanned the heading on the flier before sweeping it off the table. It was an invitation-only industry cocktail, with proceeds going to charity. It left me puzzled that he wanted me there, but I didn't question it. Whatever the boss wanted, the boss got.

"Okay. Is there anything else you need?" I asked.

"Yes. There's an emergency board meeting in an hour. I want you front and center, taking notes."

I nodded, reaching for my tablet. "Of course, Sir."

Our gazes met again. "Before the meeting, I need you to organize the room set up and ensure there are enough refreshments for everyone."

"Okay, will do. Anything else?"

"That's all."

I got up from the seat, knowing his eyes followed me as I walked out. A smile tugged my lips apart as I closed the door. The meeting didn't go half as badly as I'd thought. In fact, it went superbly well. Mr. Madden didn't hate me. Point scored. It was enough to lighten my footsteps as I started my day.

I proceeded with getting the conference room ready for the meeting, despite feeling like a glorified server while I did so. This wasn't exactly how I imagined my first job would be, but my mom was right; there was no shame in starting from the bottom. Half an hour later, I stood by the door of the meeting room, pleased with how perfect the set-up was.

I returned to my desk and spent the next half an hour sorting Mr. Madden's emails, flagging the ones that needed his urgent attention. I was so caught up with work I didn't hear him approach. A loud squeal left my lips when his hand touched my shoulder.

"Meeting room. Now," he ordered; his tone icy again.

I shot up from my desk, grabbed my tablet and followed him, almost tripping to keep up with his long strides.

We arrived at the conference room as a tall, dark middle-aged man approached from the other side. Mr. Madden stiffened, his steely eyes giving me a warning look before shifting past me.

"The elusive Jax Madden," the gentleman greeted, his tone as bright as his face. "Imagine having to call a board meeting just to see your face."

"You always know where to find me, George. The problem is, you want me to roll out the red carpet, and I have no time for that."

George chuckled. "It doesn't have to be red, Madden." At Mr. Madden's deadpan expression, George laughed harder, patting his back. "Come on. Loosen up a little."

"I can't loosen up when you're wasting my time. Why the emergency meeting?"

"You'll find out soon enough." George's eyes shifted to me, his gaze roaming my face. "And who do we have here?"

"This is my assistant, Ms. Reynolds," he replied firmly, his face still blank. "Ms. Reynolds, this is our chairman, Mr. George Andino."

"Hmm... pleasure to meet you, Ms. Cambridge." His leery gaze dropped, taking in my figure.

I forced a smile, my skin crawling from his perusal. "Nice to meet you too."

Mr. Madden's jaw tightened, the look in his eyes deadly as he gestured ahead. "This way," he said, moving off.

I followed him into the conference room, wondering where that look came from or what it meant. Soon enough, the boardroom was filled with mostly men, all of whom were impeccably dressed, fit for the front page of a magazine. Mr. Madden sat at the head of the table, radiating confidence with those reading glasses that made him look so good. I forced myself to look away, unlocking the tablet and opening the notes app.

George Andino cleared his throat, a sign to start the meeting. "I'm aware you're a busy man, Madden, so we won't take much of your time. We called this meeting to discuss the company's dismal performance. Last quarter's revenue was an embarrassment that should never happen again."

Mr. Madden's eyes slowly swept around the table, giving every member a stare. "I agree wholeheartedly, George, but please be reminded, it took them years to run this company to the ground. I've only been here a year now. I'm not a miracle worker, but I promise to turn this company around in due time."

Around the table, heads nodded in approval to Mr. Madden's response, but he still seemed uptight. His hand tightened around his pen, a slight frown scrunching the skin between his brows.

"What we need is something new," a board member said, stealing my attention. "A fresh invention that will resurrect this dying company."

"I assure you, I'm on it," Mr. Madden said tightly.

"In the meantime, I suggest we do a rebranding exercise. It worked a few years back. I believe it can work again," another board member offered.

"Won't that be like putting a bandage on a bullet wound? That won't actually fix the problem," I heard myself saying, regretting the words as soon as they left my mouth.

The room grew silent except for the soft creaking of chairs as everyone turned to look at me, including Mr. Madden, who seemed even tenser than before.

"Who's this again?" another board member rudely asked.

"This is Ms. Cambridge, Madden's assistant," George cut in. "And she's actually right. All we're doing is putting a temporary fix on the problem. What this company needs is some job cuts if it's going to survive."

My eyes widened as I glanced at Mr. Madden, who showed little emotion. "No one is losing their jobs, George," he said. "At least, not without true cause."

"We understand you need time to turn the company around, but we're running out of options. Our shareholders expect returns on their investments; we can't let them down. The hemorrhaging is out of control. You're losing money, and so are we. Do you see where I'm going with this? Something has to give," George said.

Mr. Madden stood, his body filling the space, power spreading from his shoulders downward. "I assure you, our shareholders will be well taken care of, as they have been since I took the helm. What I will not tolerate is the blatant disregard for my time, time that could be spent doing constructive work. The next time you want an update on the company's performance, email my assistant," he said, gesturing to me.

All eyes turned to me, and my face heated. I dropped my eyes to the screen, typing in a few notes.

"Have a great day, ladies and gentlemen," Mr. Madden said coolly. "Ms. Reynolds, the meeting's over. Let's go.

A few scoffs and murmurs floated, following us out. Once again, I scurried to keep up with my boss, his long strides even more forceful now. We got to my desk, and I expected him to keep walking on, but he stopped, turning to me.

"I don't pay you for your opinion, Ms. Reynolds," he hissed, his eyes fiercely narrowed.

I swallowed. "I'm sorry. The words just flew out."

"Pull a stunt like that again, and you're out. Understood?" he snapped.

"Loud and clear, Sir," I mumbled, shame filling my insides. I moved around to my seat and powered on my computer, my face still hot, my fingers trembling as I logged onto the network. It took me an instant to notice him still standing there. I glanced up, glimpsing a flash of remorse on his face before it disappeared. A soft sigh left his lips, so low I almost didn't hear it, then he walked away, his broad back disappearing as he softly shut the door behind him.

Once it closed, I leaned back in the seat, palming my face with a groan. Imagine, this day started so well. I even got a tiny smile from him. Now, we'd slid back to square one, back to the broody, cold atmosphere and the eggshells everywhere I walked.

Two months, three weeks to go.

I couldn't wait.

Chapter 8

Jax

I gave the doorman a genuine smile when he opened the front door of my apartment building, but the smile disappeared as I crossed the porcelain-tiled lobby toward the private elevator that led to my penthouse suite. It was almost eight when I shut down my computer at work, but instead of the usual exhaustion, there was high-dose adrenaline running through my veins.

The upbeat energy had nothing to do with work, well, not quite. There was something about Alyssa Reynolds that stripped every ounce of weariness away, giving me a surge of vigor caffeine could not provide.

I exited the elevator with a sigh, remembering her expression when I snapped at her earlier. Regret followed me into my apartment, and I pulled off my tie and threw it on the sofa, raking my hands through my hair. We'd made such progress this morning, getting on good ground. I even noticed how relaxed she was in that conference room. Now we were back to square one, back to the discomfort in her eyes, the stiffness in her body, her downright fear of me. She spent the entire day steering clear of me, keeping her distance even when we were in the same room. Maybe that was a good thing. Based on my increasing attraction to her, it was best she stayed away from me.

My body burned for Alyssa. Fighting that need was harder than I imagined it would be. I thought the workplace policy would be enough to keep me grounded, but it made me want her more.

There were very few things in life I'd yearned for and hadn't achieved. In time, I'd let my yearning go and moved on. With Alyssa, I had a feeling it wouldn't be that easy. She'd left an impression on me since the first time we met, and after our reunion, her effect on me had become even more pronounced. But the reality remained; she was right within my grasp but impossible to touch.

I needed her out of my system. Purged from my head. I wanted to see her and feel nothing. There was only one way to fix that.

My jaw tightened with my decision. Grunting, I pulled my phone from my pocket and dialed a number. Carrie James was an investment banker I'd met in a bar six months ago, and we'd been having casual hookups ever since. She answered on the first ring, her voice doing little to ease the fire blazing through me.

"Hey, baby," she crooned.

"I need you," I replied at once. "Be here in fifteen."

"I'll be there," came her quick response. I used the time to take a shower, and as I dried off, I heard the doorbell. I wrapped a robe around me and made my way downstairs, opening the door to find the gorgeous brunette with a seductive smile on her face. She wore a thick, belted coat, and without guessing, I knew what was underneath.

I pulled her inside and clamped my mouth to hers, the whimper from her lips stirring me. She clung to me, using her heels to close the door behind us.

We broke the kiss, and she led the way upstairs, giggling as she tugged at my robe and ran, her hair bouncing against her back. Once we got to the bedroom, she opened the coat, pulling it over her shoulders, revealing enticing red lingerie. Carrie's body was a dream – just as perfect as a plastic surgeon's catalogue, one of the most stunning I'd ever seen.

I untied my robe, watching the hunger filling her face as she took me in. Like a kid happy to see an ice cream truck, she dashed to me, kissing me with that same hunger, her hands trailing along the length of my cock, which hardened at her touch.

She dropped to her knees and massaged my length, gently squeezing my balls before she opened up her mouth and took me in. I clenched my teeth and snapped my eyes shut as her warm, soft mouth explored me. I expanded in her mouth with each squelching suck until I was solid, enjoying every moment of having my flesh inside her mouth.

I wondered if Alyssa would ever do such a thing— if she possessed enough fire to even try. What I wouldn't give to have her small mouth wrapped around me each night, sucking me just like this, her daring eyes looking up at me as I fucked her mouth.

Fuck.

I shouldn't be thinking about her. Especially not now.

Gripping the back of Carrie's head, I thrust deeper into her mouth, closing my eyes as the gurgling sounds captivated my senses. She clung onto my butt and cleared a path for her throat as I rammed myself vigorously inside her. I bared my teeth as her body stiffened from a gag, and I eased back, letting her up for air.

"The bed. Now," I ordered, and she immediately moved to obey.

I walked to the night table and pulled out a condom, slipping it on. Carrie reclined on the bed, watching me, lipstick smearing her chin. She raised her knees to her chest as I approached, her flesh in complete view, dripping wet and ready for me.

I climbed onto the bed and positioned myself in front of her, tracing my thumb across her hardened clit. Her body shuddered from the action, a soft moan leaving her lips. Foreplay had always been a huge deal. Usually, I'd tease her a little longer until she begged for me to fill her, but tonight I wanted a quick release. I wanted to get Alyssa Reynolds off my mind. Now. Screw the kissing and caressing. I needed to fuck my assistant from my system.

I shoved my cock inside Carrie in one hard thrust, her eyes popping open as she gasped. Seconds later found her whimpering, her body writhing on the bed as she begged for more.

"Harder, Jax!" she exclaimed, and I increased my pace, my head bowed as I watched my length slipping back and forth inside her. Her mouth formed an 'O' and her lashes fluttered as pleasure rocked her body. She was beautiful— the perfect view for a man as he fucked a woman, but tonight, she wasn't the vision I saw. In my mind, Alyssa had taken her place. I heard Alyssa's soft moans, her nails digging into my back, her flesh hugging my cock...

Goddamn.
This isn't working. Not even a little.

I pulled out and shifted on the bed. "On your knees for me, baby."

Carrie quickly did as I asked, her back perfectly arched with her ass aimed at me, the perfect picture of her pussy below.

She moaned as I rubbed myself up and down her flesh, clutching the sheet when I entered her with one deep thrust, her flesh parting to accommodate me. I gripped her ass and squeezed her flesh as I slammed into her over and over. Her pussy grew even wetter with each stroke, and her cries got even louder, but I didn't let up. I couldn't. That sexy, hazel-eyed girl still occupied my mind.

Carrie slipped to her stomach, her cries now muffled in the pillows as I rutted inside her. Her body shuddered, her walls clamping around me even tighter. She came hard, my name echoing off the walls as she climbed her high. I finally slowed, the pleasure increasing as I filled the sheath around my length.

Still buried inside Carrie, I wiped at my brow and muttered a curse. I slapped her on the ass before I finally pulled out and fell to the bed.

She giggled – a complete mess now. She snuggled up to me, but I couldn't yet find the breath to tell her not to. This wasn't the arrangement. We were friends with benefits; no softness, no romance.

"You can lose the condom sometimes, y'know," she whispered, kissing my ear. "I want to feel you bare inside me."

As much as that made my cock twitch, I knew better. "I don't think so, Carrie," I replied.

She sighed. "I know we had an agreement, Jax, but I can offer you more than a good time."

Damn it. Here we go. I should've known it was only a matter of time. Women like Carrie—successful, independent, confident—they always wanted more, even if they pretended otherwise. I'd hoped she was an anomaly. Guess I was wrong.

I got off the bed to discard the used condom and grab my robe. "I'm not looking for more. You know that, Carrie."

She rolled her eyes as she got from the bed. "Yeah, not from me."

"What does that mean?" I asked.

Carrie came up to me, her gaze sweeping over my face. "Is there someone else?"

My brows furrowed. "If there is, that's none of your business, Carrie. You and I aren't a thing."

"Maybe not, but we promised to be honest with each other, right?"

I exhaled a frustrated breath, wishing I'd just masturbated instead. "What do you want from me, Carrie?"

"I want you to tell me the truth. You've been acting differently. I couldn't quite figure out what it was, but I do now. You've hardly called me in the past week. Even the sex is different. There was no foreplay. You were in such a hurry to get it over with. Before tonight, you were always eager – like you couldn't get enough of me. For a second, I blamed myself, but it's clearly someone else. It's like you're trying to get someone out of your system."

It impressed me how she hit the nail on the head, but I didn't show it. Instead, I walked to the drawer for a fresh pair of boxers.

She scoffed. "You can't even deny it."

I clenched my teeth. "We had an arrangement, and that included no feelings or personal talk," I bit out.

"And I was stupid enough to think that would change," she choked, her eyes now filled with tears.

Jesus. I didn't need the theatrics. Not with the emotions still swirling inside me.

"Carrie–"

"You know what, fuck you, Jax. I got the message loud and clear!" she exclaimed, grabbing her things and leaving the room.

Not bothering to chase her, I waited in the bedroom until she got dressed downstairs. The loud slamming of my front door made it clear how mad she still was.

I'd give her time to cool down, then send her a heartfelt apology along with a bouquet and a diamond bracelet. After what just transpired, our arrangement could no longer go on. There were too many potential complications. Besides, Carrie deserved a man who was all in.

I got ready for bed, and as I slipped under the covers, I realized one thing. Tonight was a waste of time. Sleeping with Carrie had done nothing to quench my thirst for Alyssa Reynolds.

A TERRIBLE MOOD ROSE with me the next morning and followed me to work. It was probably written all over my face because of how the staff scrambled when I entered the building.

I chided myself for being later than usual because it meant seeing Ms. Reynolds before I entered my office. Since she was mostly the reason for my bad mood, I wasn't so keen on the notion, although my silly longing for her contradicted that thought.

The elevator opened up and gave me a clear view to my office door, Ms. Reynolds' desk right outside. My body hummed with awareness, my hands forming into fists when I realized I was right. Alyssa Reynolds was already in, but that wasn't the worse part. She had company. Blake Kinley, the new hire.

He leaned against her desk, making her blush with something he'd said. I knew he had a thing for her. I sensed it last Friday when I saw them together. The childish part of me considered not hiring him at all. One look at his resume changed my mind. Kinley's skills could add value to my company in due time.

Still, I fought against the urge to grab his collar and march his ass through the front door, especially when I saw how Ms. Reynolds stared at him like he was the only man in the world. I couldn't have her. I knew that. It angered the shit out of me. She could never be mine and seeing her being entertained by another man only worsened my temper.

I gripped my bag strap so tightly; I feared it would make me bleed. Each footstep felt like it weighed a ton, blood pounding in my ears.

None of them noticed me, even when I drew close enough. They were so entranced with each other, and my appearance did nothing to change that. I cleared my throat, and Ms.

Reynolds' head turned, her smile vanishing, the color instantly leaving her face.

"My office, now," I seethed, not breaking my movement. I heard the shuffling behind me as she scrambled from her seat. Not looking back, I walked into my office, leaving the door open behind me.

I dropped my bag on the desk and turned toward the entrance as I waited for her. Soon enough, she appeared, closing the door with a soft click behind her. I took in the silk top she wore, the hem tucked into her snug little skirt that showed every delectable curve. Her hair was pinned up again, and I hated it. I hated how the corporate policy forced this level of professionalism. I wanted to see it down, framing her cute face—a face that seemed somewhat brighter today. It didn't take me long to realize she had makeup on. The beauty mark right above her glossy lips was almost invisible now, which aggravated me. That was one of my favorite features. Was she dressing up for *Kinley?*

"Yes, Sir?" her silky voice came, reminding me of the reason I summoned her.

"I thought the rules were clear about fraternizing in the workplace," I said.

A wrinkle formed right between her brows. "Blake and I are just friends," she said, an edge to her voice.

It was hard to concentrate with her scent seeping into my senses. I tried to ignore my body's response to her, but fuck, it was a struggle. "Are you? It didn't seem that way to me, and I'm sure everyone else would agree," I snapped.

"I don't care what anyone thinks," she blurted, catching me off guard, irritation filling her face. She did little to hide her emotions. "I won't go around justifying my association with every guy I talk to. I'm aware of the company policy, Mr. Madden."

"You are treading on thin ice here, Ms. Reynolds," I drawled, hiding my surprise.

She raised her hands before flopping them to her sides. "If this means losing my job, then so be it. Don't assume I'm easy because of one silly mistake I made."

"I didn't say you were easy."

"You implied it," she huffed, folding her arms on her chest. "Sir."

What happened to that tense, scared-looking girl who dashed from my office yesterday? Where did she go?

"Is that all, Mr. Madden?" she asked curtly. "I have work to do."

"Be sure that's all you do, Ms. Reynolds. If I catch you flirting with Kinley, I'll put a strike on your record," I threatened.

"That's not fair—" she stopped herself, releasing a frustrated breath.

"No. Finish your sentence," I said firmly.

She bit her lips, determination in her eyes. "You're being unreasonable, Mr. Madden. How does flirting with someone affect how I do my job?"

It didn't, of course, but just thinking of Blake making her blush, something I could never do, made me see red. "Just get back to work, Ms. Reynolds. We're done with this conversation."

"You didn't answer my question. Why is flirting against the rules?" she asked, still determined.

On an impulse, I moved toward her, surprised when she didn't move. She didn't even flinch when I pulled her to me, my hands slipping around the small of her waist.

"Because flirting leads to fucking, Ms. Reynolds, and I don't want Kinley fucking you," I mumbled against her ear, her responding moan making me hard.

"Why?" she breathed, lifting her head to stare into my face. Her small body pressed against mine, her perfume like a drug. She was soft, perfect—

"Because you're mine," I whispered, giving into the urge to run my nose along her neck, taking a deep drag of her intoxicating scent. My cock hardened in my pants, pressing against her stomach. I expected her to push me off, run to HR even, but she released a soft moan and rolled her body. White-hot pleasure ran through me. I gripped the back of her head, pulling back to stare into her face.

There was no fear. No discomfort. Just blazing lust. I moved my head closer to hers, almost like a magnetic force pulling me in. She pressed on her tiptoes, her soft lips meeting mine. Perfect as I'd imagined; soft and sweet and incredibly addicting. Heat spurred within my body, settling in my groin.

But as my tongue sparred with hers and the hunger grew tenfold inside me, my cell phone rang.

Alyssa quickly pulled away, her eyes wide as she stared at me. I swallowed, wanting to hold her again – never wanting this moment to end.

"Oh, my God," she whispered, realization dawning on her face.

The cell phone kept pealing. I wanted to smash it against the wall.

"What did we just do?" she lamented, palming her cheeks.

"Hold on," I told her, reaching for the cell phone.

"No. I have to go," she said, her voice sounding slightly hoarse.

Before I could say another word, she was out the door, her scent lingering behind. I reached for the phone as the call ended, and reality sunk in as I tried calling back.

What the hell did I just do?

"Holy fuck."

Chapter 9

Alyssa

"Are you okay?" Blake asked from across the table in the café where we were having lunch.

I glanced up from the chicken salad in front of me, meeting his concerned stare. I didn't notice I'd drifted off until he asked the question. "Yeah, I am. Sorry... were you saying something?"

"No, but I'm starting to wonder if I was too forward with asking to join you for lunch," he replied. "You seem uncomfortable."

I shook my head. "No, it's not you."

"But it's something, right?" He reached across the table and took my hand. "We hardly know each other, but you can talk to me, Alyssa."

No, I can't. In fact, I can't tell anyone about what just happened. Mr. Madden kissed me, and I kissed him back. I'll lose my job if this gets out.

"How did it go with Mr. Madden this morning?" he asked. "I almost had a heart attack when he came up behind us. Thought I'd get canned for sure."

"Why? We weren't doing anything."

"I know, but did you see the look he gave me? Shit, like he wanted to murder me."

"He looks at everyone like that," I replied, my pulse tripping.

"I guess... he didn't give any flack for it, did he?"

I shrugged. "No. He was just being his usual asshole. Nothing to worry about."

Blake's shoulders relaxed as he dug into lunch, but my body remained tense throughout. I struggled to concentrate on our conversation, making me regret agreeing to have lunch with him. How could I think about anything but the kiss Jax Madden and I shared? My body still tingled at the memory, my cheeks heating as I recalled his hard cock pressed against my belly. I couldn't believe it had happened, and more than anything, I didn't even know what to make f it. What did he mean when he said I was his? Was that some alpha type of thing – a way of exerting dominance? Did Jax have feelings for me? There were too many questions and not enough answers, but although I would never admit this out loud, I'd enjoyed every moment of that kiss. Every moment of feeling like I was his, no matter how fleeting. I wanted to experience that again, but I wouldn't. It was a moment of insanity on our part. Jax Madden would never touch me again.

"I'm glad we're doing this," Blake said, pulling me from my thoughts. "Maybe we could make this a regular thing."

"We'll see." I don't want Blake to get any ideas about us. He's a good-looking guy but not my type. "So what's it like working for my mom?" I asked, lifting a forkful of food.

"It's awesome. She's really cool, and I'm not saying that because she's your mom. I'm quite lucky." He smirked. "Can't say the same for all of us. Some of us have bosses from hell."

I chuckled, rolling my eyes at him. "Whatever. Any ideas for new tech?"

"None that I've been briefed on as yet, but I've been working on software of my own. It's something that will shake the industry. I hope."

My brows raised. "Sounds amazing!"

He shook his head. "Glad you think so. Mr. Madden sure didn't."

"Really? What happened?"

"I wanted to pitch the idea to him, hoping the company would fund the prototype, but he didn't even give me the time of day. From what I heard, Stag Tech could use all the help it can get. I don't know why he's not open to new ideas. Older folks are so set in their ways."

"He's not that old," I replied, my response coming out sharper than I intended.

"I said *older*, not old. Let's face it, Alyssa. Mr. Madden is a dinosaur."

He laughed out loud, but I didn't join in. I didn't know why his response offended me so much, especially when I knew there was nothing old about Jax Madden. Definitely not the way he kissed, the firmness of his grip on me, that hard body of his...

Nope. Definitely not old.

The clicking of the opening front door stole my attention, and I glanced to the right as Mr. Madden stepped inside. My heart raced as I watched him, remembering our encounter just hours ago. He headed straight to the cashier's station and placed his order. My breath paused as his eyes searched the café. I should've looked away, but it was like something kept me frozen in place, and it remained that way until our gazes locked.

His eyes softened for a split second, then they shifted, hardening again as they landed beside me. I saw the clench in his jaw as he looked away, impatiently tapping his fingers on the counter while waiting. When the barista finally brought his order, he took it and left without glancing our way.

HE SPENT THE ENTIRE day locked in his office, communicating his orders to me over the phone. His actions left me frustrated, especially after what happened earlier that day. Did he regret making that move on me, or were his actions an attempt to fight his attraction to me?

I forced the frustration away and focused on work until it was time to head home. In the middle of packing my bag, the office phone rang. Seeing his extension on the screen made me grab the phone in a heartbeat, placing it to my ear.

"Mr. Madden?"

"My office, Ms. Reynolds," came his stiff order.

My shaking hand replaced the phone to its cradle, and I hurried to his office, closing the door behind me much harder than I intended. God, I was so nervous. Mr. Madden looked up from his desk and met my gaze. I hoped he didn't notice how terrified I was.

"Have a seat," he said, his tone still tight.

My butt gingerly hit the cushioned seat, my fingers gripping the handles. He relaxed in his chair, linking his fingers in front of him.

"I'm sorry about what happened earlier. I shouldn't have kissed you," he said, his words firm.

I bit my lower lip with a vigorous nod, disappointment running through me. "Got it, loud and clear, Sir."

"Good. You can go, Ms. Reynolds. See you tomorrow."

Annoyed at his icy dismissal, I got up from the seat, turning to go, then doubling back. "You could've told me this over the phone, Sir."

His brows lifted. "Pardon me?"

"You summoned me to your office for a one-liner that could've been communicated over a phone call."

"Phone lines are sometimes compromised. I don't want anything coming back to bite me in the ass."

I slowly nodded at his valid point, but another thought made me pause. "Why did you kiss me?"

His expression froze, then he sucked in a deep breath and slowly released it. "A temporary moment of insanity," he finally replied.

"Was it that bad?" I asked.

He closed his eyes, his lips a tight line across his face. "You need to leave, Ms. Reynolds."

He opened his eyes, and I saw the turmoil there. The dilemma. The guilt. For some reason, it fueled me, pushing me forward. "Be honest with me, Jax." I used his first name on purpose because it seemed appropriate in that moment. "It wasn't bad, was it? Did you feel something like I did?"

Fury flashed across his face, and he sat upright. "Do you understand what you're asking me to admit? What the implications could be? I'm a hypocrite, Ms. Reynolds. I created and enforced a policy that I broke. How do you think that makes me look? No one will respect me if they find out what we did."

"I'm not asking you to shout it from the rooftops. We're alone in this room. I need to know I'm not the only one losing my mind from something that felt so perfectly amazing and—" I palmed my cheeks with a loud gasp, knowing I treaded deep waters that could cost my job, but I didn't care in that moment. "—so right."

"Right?" He shook his head. "God, you have no idea what you're talking about, *young* lady."

"I'm not too young," I threw back, catching his subtle message. "I know when a man wants me. I know *you* want me. I felt your cock against my—"

"Enough!"

My body jerked as Jax flew up from his chair, and I backed off as he came around the table, moving to me. He stopped right in front of me and crossed his arms on his chest, his powerful biceps bulging under the impeccable suit.

"Get your head out of the clouds, *Alyssa*," he bit out. "This is real life, where there are rules put in place to keep things in order. Messing with that order only causes complications that ruin lives. Stag Technologies is in deep shit because people broke those rules. You're not a kid anymore. This isn't high school. You don't get to be a rebel here and then go off unscathed. You certainly won't get to be a rebel with me."

My heart dropped to the floor of my stomach, and tears pricked my eyes. "I'm not a rebel," I whisper.

"Prove it. Keep your head down, do your job, and for God's sake, pretend like this morning didn't happen."

I lifted my chin, raising myself to full height. "Understood, Mr. Madden. I'm sorry. This will never happen again."

"Good." He jerked his head toward the door. "You can go."

I whipped around, making haste to the door, and closing it softly behind me. The tears remained at bay until I grabbed my bag and made my way to the car. They escaped the instant I closed the door, reducing me to a sobbing, pitiful mess.

DINNER WAS ALREADY in full swing when I finally composed myself enough to drive home. I got in to find Mom around the stove, stirring something in a saucepan that smelled like heaven.

She whipped around as I dropped my purse to the counter. "Hey, honey. Thought you would've been home earlier," she said, still stirring the pot.

"Had a meeting with the boss," I replied. At her soft gasp, I clarified. "Nothing serious. Just a little... reinforcement."

"I see." She frowned, leaning in. "Were you crying?"

I shook my head, forcing a smile. "No, just my allergies acting up. What are you cooking?"

The frown did not leave her face, but she went back to stirring the pot. "Short ribs and mash."

I closed my eyes and inhaled a whiff of the aroma. "Ugh, I haven't had that in a while. Can't wait."

She wiped her hands and pulled a bottle of wine from the cabinet, followed by two glasses. "You're just in time; all I have to do now is plate it." She slid the bottle across the counter toward me.

I slipped off the stool and went to get an opener while Mom busied herself with sharing. Shortly after, we got comfortable around the island in our kitchen, eating and drinking wine.

"Besides that meeting with Mr. Madden, how was work?" she asked, dipping the fork into the mountain of mashed potatoes. "We've both been so busy I haven't even had the time to ask."

I took a mouthful of the red wine, thinking of that steamy encounter. If only Mom knew how work was, she'd have a heart attack.

"I er— it's going fine. Better than I expected," I replied with a tight smile.

"See, I told you it wouldn't be so bad. I heard you already made a new friend too. Blake told me about having lunch with you today." She winked at me.

I snorted. "Blake is just a friend, Mom, and he's definitely not my type," I murmured, taking another drink.

She straightened in her chair. "You were a handful in high school, especially with the boys, so I never thought I'd actually say this. Honey, you need to start dating again. It's not healthy to be alone at your age. There are so many good-looking young men in this town."

"I heard you, Mom."

"Unless you're into girls."

"No, I'm not. I just haven't found my person, that's all," I said.

"Well, to do that, you'd actually have to date, sweetheart."

"I get it, and I will."

"And Blake seems like a nice guy – definitely smart."

I pulled in a breath. "Mom..."

She held up her hands in surrender. "Okay, okay, I'll stop meddling in your love life."

"Speaking of love lives, why don't *you* try dating again?" I questioned.

Mom blushed and fanned me off. "Please, I'm almost fifty years old, sweetheart. The last thing I want is to enter the dating pool again."

"It could be fun."

"I suppose," she cleared her throat. "But I have so much to do right now. Tech is under high pressure now at work. I'm even surprised I found the time to cook this dinner."

"I sat in on a board meeting the other day, and it doesn't look good, Mom."

She sighed. "I know."

"Do you guys have a plan?"

"We're working on something, but I don't know. We'll see," she said. "And while we're on the subject, I'm thinking of inviting Mr. Madden over for dinner on the weekend."

I froze. "What?"

Her brows furrowed. "Why do you seem surprised, honey? I've had coworkers over for dinner before."

"Only, he's not just any coworker, Mom. He's your boss," I reminded.

"So? I invited Tony Bancroft many times in the past, and he was my boss. I even remember you being excited when I had him over."

"Tony was a nice guy." *At least to my mom's face.* "Mr. Madden is..." I remembered his rejection, and my heart twisted in my chest. "... an asshole."

Mom covered her mouth, her eyes wide with shock.

"Relax, Mom. We're in a safe space."

"Just don't let that slip in public. Jax Madden is a powerful man," she warned.

Yes, I knew exactly how powerful he was. I remembered the force of his grip as he kissed me with that skillful mouth—

Ugh. I need to stop thinking about how amazing that was. He doesn't want me. It was a stupid mistake.

"Holy crap," Mom murmured, swiping her phone screen. "This weekend is a no-no. There's a company event on Saturday night."

"I know. The industry cocktail. Mr. Madden invited me."

Her brows lifted in surprise. "He invited you? That's a first."

"What do you mean?"

"It's a company event, but it's a limited invitation. Each department head gets to take a plus one. CEOs usually invite a senior executive or a board member. Never an assistant. This is good for you, for it's a chance to network. Yet, it's still odd."

"I see." Not wanting to read too much into it, I pushed the thought away. "Who's your plus one?"

"I'm sitting it out this year, so I gave my invite to Janet, the supervisor in my department. She's taking Blake as her plus one." She grinned, winking at me. "Maybe you can save a dance for him."

"You're hell-bent on this matchmaking, aren't you?" I replied, chuckling.

"Only if it's what you want, honey. Your happiness is all that matters to me."

I smiled, giving my hand to her as she reached for it, giving it a gentle squeeze.

Chapter 10

Jax

My workplace was now a subsidiary of hell. Nothing short of torture. For eight hours of the day, I lived on the verge of insanity. The nights weren't better, either. How was it that someone could penetrate my soul like this? Why the fuck did she affect me so much? How could a single encounter five years ago create such an attachment to someone I couldn't erase from my mind?

Fuck!

There were so many factors working against us. It wasn't just me being her boss. There was the age gap to consider. Dating a woman almost twice my age was a move that would raise every eyebrow in my circle. Not that it was a crime, but there was an unspoken rule no one in my circle dared to break. She could be my daughter—well, barely, if I'd gotten a kid at twenty years old.

The more I tried to resist my attraction to her, the worse my desire became. Kissing her was a huge mistake because it triggered an addiction so strong my body craved for the next fix.

I raked my fingers through my hair, reflecting on our last conversation and how quickly it went south. I didn't expect her challenge. Her comment threw me completely off guard.

"I know when a man wants me. I know you want me. I felt your cock against my—"

Fuck.

Fuck, fuck, fuck.

I was in deep trouble.

Would it hurt to give into temptation just once? Could I settle for just one taste? The answers were yes and no. Nothing could ever happen between us, not even a fling.

Yet when Ms. Reynolds walked into my office the following morning, my resolve immediately slipped away. Her outfit didn't help one bit. The skirt that hugged her curves, the blouse that gave me a peek of her cleavage, those heels that made her shapely legs even sexier than before, even her dark hair that she wore in her usual up-do seemed sexy to me. Her lipstick seemed brighter this morning, triggering the memory of that kiss.

"You wanted to see me, Sir?" she asked, her eyes on the wall behind my head.

"Come in, Ms. Reynolds. Have a seat."

I slid my iPad across the table to her, and she caught it, peering at the screen. "That's my latest expense report. I need you to remove the extra-curricular expenses and give me the updated costs by the end of the day."

She nodded, eyes still locked on the screen. "I'll get right on it. Anything else?"

Yes. I want to pull those pins and watch your hair fall. To run my fingers through it, to grab a handful as I taste those lips again. I want you on all fours on this desk, taking my cock. I want to hear you screaming my name as you come.

"That's all," I replied out loud.

She quickly rose, moving briskly to the door, her ass swinging as she went. My hands curled on my lap, and I imagined them palming her cheeks as I fucked her—

Jesus.

This can't go on.

"Ms. Reynolds."

Almost through the door, she turned with a questioning stare. "Yes, Sir?"

"I want you to stay behind after work. There's something we need to discuss."

She swallowed, a slight movement in her slender neck, a flash of hope crossing her face. "Okay."

She remained in place for another second, our gazes locked, my raging boner tempting me to yank her inside and spend the rest of the afternoon between her thighs.

"That's all."

With that, she turned and left, and I threw my head against the back of the seat, muttering a curse.

IT HAD TO BE DONE. There was no other option. But the closer I got to the end of the workday, the greater my anxiety. I got up from my desk and walked to the window overlooking the busy city. This wasn't how I'd imagined things would be when I took over the troubled company. One year later, and there was no sign of the change I'd hoped to bring. To top it off, I now contended with an attraction to a woman I couldn't have. A total distraction. How many hours had I wasted thinking about her, wanting her, fighting my feelings for her?

Something had to be done. It was time to think with my head and not my dick. I should've done this from the very moment I saw her again. I shouldn't have hired her. It was the worst decision I'd ever made.

Fifteen minutes past five, her knock came at the door, and my heart twisted in my chest. *Here the fuck goes nothing.* I scrubbed my face, moving away from the window.

"Come!" I called.

The door popped open, and she slipped through, closing it behind her.

"Have a seat, Ms. Reynolds," I instructed, watching as she moved to comply.

I returned to my chair and cleared my throat, giving her my full attention. "I need you to hand in your resignation letter by the end of the week."

Her eyes widened. "What?"

"You heard me, Ms. Reynolds."

"Why?" she asked, her brows furrowing.

I inhaled sharply. "I made a mistake –"

"Is this about the kiss?"

"Yes. We can't continue with a working relationship, not after what happened."

"I don't understand. It meant nothing to you. Why does it matter if we work together?"

I stared at her, thinking of a response that made sense. Thinking of a lie.

She scoffed, leaning back in her seat. "You don't want to work with me because you feel something."

For a moment, I considered denying it. I opened my mouth to do so, but the words did not come. "It doesn't matter what I feel, Alyssa. This was a mistake I'm trying to fix."

"A mistake." She scoffed again, shaking her head. "What was so wrong about it?"

"We've had this discussion before. The rules, Alyssa. You're an employee, and I'm —I'm twice your age."

"Only by twenty years. Besides, I'm an adult," she fired back.

I shook my head as she leaned in. "I'm a woman, Jax."

I gritted my teeth, at a complete loss for words. My head spun; every inch of my body now alive. She got up from her chair, and my eyes latched onto her as she moved to my side, her sweet, intoxicating scent adding more fuzz to my brain.

"The truth is, I haven't stopped thinking about you since that night in your hotel room." She licked her lips, sighing softly. "And I know it's wrong— I get that it's against the rules, but Jax... no one has to know."

Holy fuck.

She spun my chair, making me face her. "Unless... unless you don't want me."

I dropped my gaze to the front of my pants. "I think it's pretty obvious that I do."

A soft moan left her lips, and she reached down, running her fingers over my erection. My hips jerked upwards, aching for more of her touch.

"I'll make it worth your while, I promise," she whispered in my ear.

Jesus. It would be easier to thread a camel through a needle's eye than say no, especially with her hand massaging my cock, her warm breath fanning my ear. My body was so tight with tension I feared it would explode. I needed release. I wanted Alyssa Reynolds. It was no use denying it anymore.

I grabbed her chin, bringing her face close to mine, our breaths mixing. "Whatever happens stays right here. Understood?"

"I promise," she replied with a vigorous nod.

Chapter 11

Alyssa

The old Alyssa had returned. Bold, carefree, not giving a shit about the rules. I wanted Jax Madden, and realizing he wanted me even more, there was nothing to stop me from making a move.

I gave myself a shoulder tap for holding out for so long. Five years was a long stretch. I'd been a good girl long enough. My craving for Jax surpassed my resolve to stay on the straight and narrow.

I touched the smooth fabric of his suit, feeling every defined muscle through it. His eyes darkened to a dark, ashy gray, telling me how much he wanted this. He wanted *me*.

Silently, my hand moved across the seams of his expensive suit, moving under and feeling more of what I craved. I swallowed as I slipped it from his shoulders and watched patiently as he shrugged it from his arms, revealing his snugly fit undershirt that covered his hard body.

I plucked at the buttons, watching his expression. He looked just about ready to pounce, his jaw set firmly.

I only saw a glimpse of his toned chest and the dark hair that covered it before he gripped my hand, the fire from his touch spreading throughout my body. He gripped the back of my head, pulling it downward. Our lips met, the contact was fierce and hungry. I kissed him eagerly, the hard strokes of his tongue filled with much passion that weakened my knees.

I moaned against his mouth, his free hand weaving through my hair as he held me in place. Arousal coursed through me, rushing to the most sensitive area on my body, soaking my panties and leaving me desperate for his cock inside me.

I pulled away with a gasp and hastened to peel off his shirt. Though I wanted a second to glory in the sight of him, I went straight for his buckle, fumbling as I tried to set him free.

Jax pushed to his feet and groped my ass, pulling me closer to him, almost knocking the wind out of me. I moaned again, feeling the hard outline of his cock pressing against my stomach. My core pooled with even more heat, hastening my fingers on his belt.

"Are you sure you want this?" he asked huskily as I pulled the zipper down.

"I've never been more certain about anything," I whispered.

His jaw clenched before he lowered his mouth to mine and kissed me so hard my knees buckled.

I yanked down his pants, trailing my hand over his front, my eyes widening at how huge he was. Jax moved me aside and cleared the top of his desk, tucking his iPad in the drawer and propping me on top. I leaned back, using my arms to brace myself, as he pulled my skirt upward, bringing it over my hips and exposing the lace panties I wore underneath. His eyes dropped to the spot between my legs, an unmistakable hunger filling their depths. He cupped my face with both hands, staring intently down at me.

"Make sure this is what you want, Alyssa because there's no going back."

I nodded, all fuzzy-brained and aroused all at once. "I want this," I said, my voice slightly shaky. "I need you."

Jax released a shuddering breath, his thumb tracing my lower lip. His free hand tugged at the waistband of my panties. The breath hitched in my throat as I eased up a little and watched as he pulled my underwear off, taking a sniff before shoving it in his pocket.

My body was on fire as he pulled me closer to the edge, kneeling in front of me. I gripped the edge of the desk and spread my thighs, heat rushing to that throbbing spot. He trailed his fingers up my thighs and stared at me unabashedly as if wanting to commit the image to memory.

"You're beautiful," he murmured, and I whimpered as his warm breath fanned my flesh.

I closed my eyes, bracing for the first lash of his tongue. My body shuddered as he licked upwards, caressing the seam with soft yet purposeful strokes. I arched my back when he lapped my clit, insurmountable pleasure running through me.

I'd read about cunnilingus in books and watched online porn, yet I'd never experienced it... until now. And it was all I imagined it to be – all that and absolutely more.

His tongue was soft yet firm as it gently bathed my flesh from top to bottom, occasionally sweeping over my hardened nub before he continued with the same cycle.

"Ohh..." I whimpered, opening my eyes and quickly closing them again when another round of pleasure swept through me. This time, it was more than licking. Jax had found my opening, and his tongue slipped right in, thrusting and exploring my walls.

"Oh, God!" I exclaimed softly, trying to spread my legs though they could go no further. My fingers tightened around the edge of the desk, and I threw my head back, completely lost in the pleasure that filled me.

Moments later, with my eyes still rolling in the back of my head, I felt the push of his finger at my entrance. His mouth was still on me, sucking my sensitive clit. I groaned, biting down on my lips as his thick digit moved inside me.

My chest rose and fell as my panting grew, the effects of his multi-tasking overwhelming me. I rocked my hips, riding his finger, prompting my release. The first wave of pleasure covered me, and I rocked my hips faster, crushing my pussy against his face.

"I'm coming, Jax!" I whispered harshly, my hips lifting off the desk when he hummed in response. My body shook as the wildest ecstasy assaulted every inch of my body.

My elbows slipped against the desk, making me land on my back, and I chuckled between my rough panting, my body now weightless. I felt so free – so good. I smiled as my eyes fluttered, Jax making an appearance over me. He wore a smug expression, his lips moist with my cum.

"That was amazing. Thank you," I breathed.

A ghost of a smile played at his lips before he reached for his shirt. My brows furrowed.

"What are you doing? Don't you want to—"

"Patience, Alyssa," he replied, doing up the buttons. "I'll see you at work tomorrow."

What the hell?

I slid off the table and had to quickly catch myself as my knees buckled. Any moment, I expected Jax to reach for me, confessing he was only fucking with my head. He didn't seem the type to joke around, though. He definitely did not want to sleep with me.

My eyes dropped to the front of his pants, seeing the proof of his arousal there. It confused and disturbed me. Here I was, a willing vessel for his pleasure, yet he didn't want to use me.

With a hard swallow, I pulled down my skirt and used my hands to comb back my hair. I probably looked a mess, but it was after-work hours, which meant there was no one but us on the executive floor, so I could head to the bathroom before I left.

His eyes were on me as I got my shoes on. I did another quick run-through of my hair before moving off. "Okay then. I guess I'll see you tomorrow," I said, walking past him and heading toward the door.

The breath caught in my throat when he pulled me back and kissed me on the lips. I moaned, pressing myself against him, but he pulled away almost at once, dismissing me with a gesture to the door. I left the office even more disturbed than when I entered. His hot-and-cold behavior didn't comfort me at all. Who would I meet when I returned to work tomorrow; the passionate man who made me come so hard just now or the ice-cold boss who wanted to stick to the rules?

Chapter 12

Alyssa

By the next morning, I was a nervous wreck, the reality of our steamy encounter catching up with me. I drove to work with my stomach filled with dread, wondering if Jax had already regretted what we did, especially with how quiet he'd been afterwards. Add that to him not fucking me: would we backslide to square one, where he would ask me to resign again, or did I have more steamy moments to look forward to?

There was a hard knot in my stomach as I reversed into a parking spot, and I knew it wouldn't go away anytime soon. Especially not in Jax Madden's company. Definitely not since we'd been intimate. His tongue had been inside me. He'd tasted my cum. I screamed his name when the climax burst inside me.

There was no going back after what we shared. Quite frankly, I didn't want it to. I wanted Jax, and the feeling was mutual. I hoped the rules wouldn't stand in our way. I certainly hoped he wouldn't fire me. How would I explain that to my mom?

The elevator doors closed, and I glanced in the mirror to my right, groaning softly as I took in my outfit; why the hell did I wear pants? They did not give easy access. Removing them would be so clumsy and time-consuming, definitely not ideal for a quickie.

I shook my head at the ambitious thought. If Jax's behavior was anything to go by, there wouldn't be a quickie any time soon.

I got to my desk and realized Jax wasn't in as yet, but I expected he would step through that door anytime soon. I tried getting busy with work but couldn't stop thinking about him. It wasn't just how good he made me feel. There was a longing for something more than just his lips on me. I wanted to know the man beneath that skillful tongue. I wondered what it would be like to wake up next to him—

No.

I shook my head, clearing the insane thought. I didn't want to know him. This was a fling, nothing else. It wasn't a healthy thing to even consider more.

Just as I'd expected, Jax arrived a few minutes later, work bag strapped over his shoulder, wearing a dark suit that contrasted his piercing grey eyes. I didn't want to make my staring obvious, but I couldn't help it. I almost pinched myself at the notion that this powerful billionaire had been between my legs yesterday, bringing me to a mind-numbing orgasm. A smile formed on my lips as he approached, my heartbeat picking up pace. I didn't know what to expect. Jax Madden was such an unpredictable man.

He confirmed it by greeting me with a cool, flat "Ms. Reynolds" as the only form of acknowledgment as he walked by. My heart deflated, then I caught myself. We were at work. There were employees moving up and down the corridor. Any changed behavior between us would arouse suspicion from anyone else around.

Regardless, part of me wanted a smile or even a wink since a kiss wasn't on the table. I held onto the hope that our after-work encounter would continue, but as the middle of the workday approached, Jax exited his office and walked up to my desk, his expression unreadable – no hint that anything had happened between us. It surprised me that he was so cool while I burned so much for him.

"I'm leaving early for a meeting. You may take the rest of the day," he informed, glancing at his watch.

My forehead wrinkled, disappointment filling me. "Er– okay..."

Our gazes held for a brief second before he gave a curt nod and left. I swallowed the lump in my throat and watched as the elevator closed with him before logging off, grabbing my bag and then leaving shortly after.

I get the message, Jax Madden. Loud and clear.

THIS IS THE LAST THING I expected, getting a call from you in the middle of the day, asking to meet up for a drink," Liz said, slipping onto the bar stool beside me. "Not that I'd ever say no to a drink, no matter what time it is."

I forced a tiny smile. Liz was a borderline alcoholic, though she would never admit it.

"Shouldn't you be at work, though? I can't imagine Jax Madden giving you time off."

The bartender placed the pre-ordered martinis in front of us, and I took a sip, welcoming the burn in my throat. "Well, he did, and I needed someone to talk to. You're the lucky victim. Prepare to have your ears chewed off."

She chuckled. "What's going on?"

I sighed. "What do you do when you start getting mixed signals from a guy?"

Liz raised a neatly sculpted brow. "Well... I usually just ghost them or cut whatever it is off," she replied with a shrug.

I shook my head. "Uh-Uh. That's not an option." At least, not for the next two months.

"What do you mean it's not an option?" Liz asked, inflamed. "The last thing you want to do is waste your time on an asshole who's unsure about what he wants. We're both better than that."

I bit my lips as I gave that some thought.

"So, who's the guy?" she prodded, and my head shot up at the question.

"Uh– nobody. The advice isn't for me. I just wanted to get your opinion," I replied, faking a smile.

Liz pursed her lips at me, clearly not convinced, making me regret saying anything. I couldn't even let my shadow in on what happened with Jax and I.

"Yeah, right," she said, scoffing.

I cleared my throat. "Remember that guy who spilled beer on me at the club? He's now working at Stag, and we've become friends. Well, kind of," I said.

"The cute guy who was totally into you? Wow, small world."

"Yeah, microscopic."

"Is he the one giving you mixed signals?"

"Um... yeah. One minute, he's hot; the next, he's treating me like I'm just another employee—I mean, co-worker. It's irritating."

"Did you talk to him about it?"

"Nah... and I'm not going to. He won't understand."

She frowned. "Forget him. What are you doing tomorrow? A friend of mine is having a party on the river, and I heard how crazy it's going to be. Crazy good, that is."

I sighed. "Sounds like fun, but I actually have this work event tomorrow." Not that I was in the mood to see Jax after he iced me out today.

Liz rolled her eyes. "Boring!"

"I know. Wish I could ditch it — which reminds me; I have to find something to wear."

Liz straightened in her chair. "Well, that I can certainly help with. What are you looking for?"

"Something formal and classy. Sexy without being desperate. You know what I mean?" Jax Madden could ice me out all he wanted, but I had a sudden perfect plan to make him melt for me.

"Hmm... I know exactly what you mean, and I know just the place — and I'll pay."

"What? Liz, you don't have to do that. Besides, I'm the one with the job."

She scoffed. "And I'm the one with more money than I can spend in this lifetime. It's no biggie. Come, let's go."

Taking one last swallow of my drink, I giggled as Liz pulled me off the stool, and I stumbled after her. As a borderline alcoholic and a certified shopaholic, this was a perfect day for my best friend.

I TRAILED MY HANDS along the racks of clothes, struggling to decide. Liz wasn't much help, either. She left my side almost immediately after we got there, but I heard her voice on the other side of the store. Undoubtedly, there would be a high pile at the cashier's counter when she got done.

I moved between the mannequins, admiring each dress carefully, still not knowing what to choose. I wanted something sexy enough to get Jax's attention, making the decision even harder. Should I choose something with a thigh-high split, a cut-out back, a deep neckline or all three? No. Way too slutty. I blew a frustrated breath, twisting a sequined dress on the hanger.

"I've never seen you so indecisive about choosing an outfit before. I thought you would've been done by now," Liz said behind me, making me jump.

I turned to meet the curious look on her face, hoping my face wasn't as red as it was hot. Clearing my throat, I returned my gaze to the clothing rack. "Well, this is my first event since working with the company. I don't want to look like a hot mess."

"Or maybe you want to impress your boss."

My head snapped back to her. "What?"

"It's him, isn't it?"

I could feel the heat rising to my cheeks. "What do you mean?"

"Mixed Signals Guy. It's your boss, right?"

I swallowed hard, glancing around me. Heaven help me if there was a co-worker in the store.

"Just admit it. I caught the slip of your tongue in the bar. Employee/co-worker," she clarified.

I sucked at lying and even more so to my best friend. "Fine. Mixed Signals Guy is my boss," I whispered. "Just keep your voice down, please."

She wiggled her brows, her eyes sparkling with humor. "When did this go down?"

"Not here!" I hissed, glancing around again.

Liz glanced around, too. "Wait a minute. Is this a secret affair?"

"Liz!"

"Damn! Okay... okay..." she trailed off and cleared her throat. "You don't have to tell me now. You can just compile everything for next weekend for our girls' night in. I want to have my popcorn ready and a glass of wine."

I rolled my eyes. "You're something else."

"And you are back, my naughty little best friend. You seduced him, didn't you?" she asked, nudging me.

"If I tell you, then I have no choice but to kill you," I joked, and she laughed.

Liz clapped her hands. "Now that I know what I'm working with, I have the perfect dress in mind, one will knock his socks off. There's no way he'll give any more mixed signals when he sees you in this."

I pressed my fingers to my temple. "Why does it feel like I'll regret saying yes?"

"Come on." She reached for my hand, pulling me to the high-fashion section of the store. "This would look so freaking good on you," she said, pulling a golden gown with beaded straps and a thigh-high split off the rack. My breath hitched in the back of my throat as I assessed every seamless inch. It was perfect.

"This is the one," Liz said, whistling.

"Perfect," I breathed, already imagining Jax's reaction.

Liz did a happy jig on our way to the cashier. She made a sudden stop, making me bump into her back. "Oh, and one more thing."

"What is it now?" I asked.

"You're going to name your firstborn baby after me."

My heart fluttered at the wishful thinking that Jax and I would share more than a fling someday. I composed myself, pushing the far-fetched notion aside. "It's not that kind of party, Liz."

"Not yet," she replied knowingly. "But I'm telling you, this dress will bring that man to his knees. Mark my word."

As I waited for the cashier to ring up the order, the crazy side of me wished—hoped Liz had an unknown gift of prophecy. I wanted Jax Madden to kneel for me.

Chapter 13

Jax

I glanced at my watch, then checked out the entrance of the ballroom, wondering why there was no sign of Alyssa yet. Granted, she was only a few minutes late, but seeing she'd never shown up late for work before, I expected no less now, regardless of this not being the same thing.

Not for the last time, I wondered if I'd made the right decision inviting her here. After what happened between us earlier in the week, having her in an environment like this was a risky move, with so many eyes on me, so many chances of my attraction to her getting noticed. I couldn't afford that secret to get out in the open, to lose anyone's respect right now. Not when I was so close to achieving my goal.

I took a sip of champagne and forced a smile, trying to focus on the conversation with the small group that surrounded me. My eyes scanned the room, taking in the laughter, and the gentle hum of chatter floating around, the scent of expensive perfume mixing and the soft clink of champagne glasses filling the air. Upbeat music played in the background, adding to the festive vibe. This wasn't my scene. Mixing shoulders with the rich and powerful was never my thing. But as a poor boy trying to make his way to the top, I understood how important networking was. Twenty-four years later, the ass-kissing had done well for me.

A woman suddenly gasped behind me, and I noticed a few heads turning toward the entrance— those being mostly middle-aged men whose faces lit up like a kid in a candy store.

I turned to see what had caught their attention and immediately froze. Alyssa Reynolds stood at the entrance, her gaze wildly scanning the room as she clutched a small purse in front of her. My fingers tightened around the stem of the glass as I took her in, as she took my breath away. She was a goddess in that golden dress, the shimmer making her skin glow. But what made my heart pause was her hair in a half up-do, some hanging in loose waves over her shoulders and down her back. I could already feel my fingers running through them. I imagined getting a firm handful as I kissed her, that sexy body pressing against me.

Alyssa timidly bit her lips and took a few steps forward, still searching the room. I didn't take my eyes off her until our gazes locked. Her face lit up, and the faintest smile curled her lips. She moved down the steps, and my eyes remained glued to her – I just couldn't look away. Not when she was the most beautiful being in the room, her dress clinging to every inch of her body, hugging every single mouth-watering curve she possessed. My gaze lowered, getting a peek of her creamy thigh that peeked from the side split.

I released a slow breath and straightened my posture, holding onto every bit of control. The guests parted like the Red Sea as she moved toward me, almost every eye on her. Why did I feel like the luckiest man alive, yet the most cursed? I shouldn't look at her like this, with this searing longing. I shouldn't be looking at her at all.

Alyssa stopped before me, and my heart stopped for a millisecond. My hands itched to touch her, so I slipped one into my pocket, the other firmly holding the glass. I arranged a neutral expression. This was no time to act like a lovesick schoolboy.

"Good evening, Mr. Madden," she greeted me with a smile, her lips a faint shade of red that looked so inviting.

Unable to help myself, I reached my hand around her back and leaned in, the scent of her cologne overpowering the rest of my will. "You look stunning," I whispered, my lips just mere inches from her jeweled ear.

Despite her makeup, I could see the blush on her cheeks when I backed away. "Thank you." She cleared her throat, gesturing to me. "You look great, too."

I subconsciously glanced down at my dark suit, which I certainly did not put any effort into. "Thank you."

"I'm sorry I'm late. I–"

I waved off her apology. "It's fine. You missed nothing." I took her arm, noticing the thrill that ran through me when we touched. "Come on. Let me introduce you to some important people."

We spent the next half an hour moving around the room, chatting with industry moguls, some of whom left Alyssa so star-struck she could hardly talk. I caught a few of them flirting with her, and I ended the conversation each time, moving her far away from them. It was a juvenile move, but I didn't care. I wanted no other man's hands on her but mine.

It was a selfish thought, too, especially when I didn't plan on touching her like that again. Alyssa was my subordinate.

I was her boss. My raging lust did not change the facts. She couldn't be mine, not even for another moment.

I made the rules. I couldn't change them because I wanted a good time.

"Why are you being so nice to me?" Alyssa asked as we moved on from the owner of a multi-billion-dollar Ad agency.

"Am I being nice?" I threw back.

She glanced sideways at me as if trying to figure me out. "You literally gave Mr. Magnus a personal recommendation if he wants to hire me in the future. Why would you do that?"

"Why wouldn't I? You're a hard worker," I pointed out.

"But I've only been working with you for two weeks—"

"Two consistent weeks," I interrupted. "You showed up for work on time, never complained about the long to-do list and always completed your work by end of day. I've been a boss for a long time, Alyssa. I know a decent worker when I see one."

She managed a quick smile as we stopped on the outskirts of the dance floor. "For a moment, I thought you were trying to get rid of me."

"I see your brain's been working overtime. Why would I want that?"

Alyssa glanced around her, then leaned in a little. "Because you've been so cold with me since we—"

"Got it." I glanced around, too, but everyone seemed preoccupied. "I've been trying to reset the boundaries, that's all."

"I thought we'd gone past that."

"Well, you thought wrong. The rules are still in place, *Ms. Reynolds*."

A slight frown pulled her lips into a tight line, and she nodded curtly.

"You do understand, don't you?" I asked.

"Can I be honest?"

I nodded. "Go right ahead."

"It's a stupid rule," she said in a half-whisper. "There shouldn't be any restrictions on romance. People should be free to love who they want."

"I see your point, but the company has been burned in the past because of that freeness, as you put it. We're trying to save the business, not burn it down," I said tightly.

"Encouraging healthy relationships won't burn it down, Mr. Madden," she replied, her tone stiff. "You made a blanket rule without considering any exceptions, and that's not fair."

"Are you looking for a healthy relationship within my company?"

A deep blush covered her cheeks, and she lifted her chin. "I might."

As I opened my mouth to query further, someone brushed against my side.

"Alyssa, thank God. I've been looking all over for you. There's literally no one in our age group here but us."

Blake Kinley moved past me—obviously not noticing me standing there—and pulled Alyssa in for a hug, one that lasted a little too long, their bodies pressed too close together. Alyssa smiled and looped her shoulders around his neck, the tension gone from her face.

I stood there watching, gritting my teeth so hard I thought they'd shatter in my mouth. I wanted to peel him off her and pound his body into the floor. I wanted to take her away from here, to show her I gave zero fucks about the rule, to show her how much I'd been aching for more than just my tongue inside her. If there was a budding romance between her and Blake, I wanted to fuck every notion of him out of her head. I wanted to leave my mark on her, one that would deter any other man.

Fuck my life. Fuck this dilemma. Fuck this asshole trying to take what's mine.

Damn it. No. She's not mine. She can never be mine.

Blake glanced at me, immediately doing a double take, his face paling when he realized it was me.

"Er– Mr. Madden. I didn't.... I didn't see you there," he stuttered, glancing back at Alyssa.

I grunted, taking another champagne flute from a passing waiter. Without saying a word, I shot Alyssa a cool glance before moving to interact with the other guests. My gaze occasionally shifted back to her, and my heart dipped when I noticed how much she enjoyed Blake's company. He made her laugh, for fuck's sake, and I lost count of how many times she touched his arm. Anger surged through me. I tried to focus on the conversation with an old business associate, but my entire focus lay across the room. From the corner of my eye, I watched as Blake stretched out his hand, his lips slowly moving. Alyssa grinned and slipped her hand into his. My chest tightened painfully. I emptied the contents of my glass down my throat as they headed to the dance floor, and as Blake pulled her in his arms, I saw red.

For the first time, I didn't think about the rules. I cared less about the opinions of the people in the room. My only aim was to recapture what I'd lost: Alyssa's attention. I wanted her eyes on me. That smile should be reserved for only me.

Blood pounded in my ears as I stormed toward the dance floor.

Chapter 14

Alyssa

I enjoyed Blake's company more than I expected, but it wasn't enough. He was too cute and funny. I wanted dark and broody. He looked charming in a navy blue suit and sneakers. I wanted hot, sexy, set-my-body-on-fire-with-one-look. Blake was soft. I wanted hard. No, he didn't do it for me.

My gaze kept shifting back to Jax, that *ding, ding, ding!* going off in my head each time. His iciness pissed me off, but it did nothing to quell my longing for him. I already missed the feel of his hand against me and the warmth of his breath against my skin when he whispered in my ear earlier.

The way he looked at me, that deep, burning gaze, the scowl that made his eyebrows bunch together, it was so fucking hot. Such a turn-on. My pussy throbbed when I imagined him coming at me, sweeping me off my feet and fucking me against the wall of a backroom somewhere. Wishful thinking, but still enough to leave my body humming with need. I'd never been this horny in my life.

Maybe I need to cut back on drinking, just so I don't lose my mind tonight.

"Hey, everything okay?" Blake asked, his hand gently touching my shoulder.

I cleared my throat and smiled. "Yeah. This isn't really my scene, but I'm trying to enjoy myself."

Blake nodded. "Yeah, mine either. You look beautiful, by the way — an absolute stunner. That dress..." He kissed his fingers. "Perfection."

I grinned, looking down at myself. "Thank you. It doesn't hurt to have a best friend with an incredible fashion sense."

He scoffed. "Please; you'd look good in a garbage bag."

"Ha! I don't think so," I replied.

"Trust me," he said seriously. "You'd look amazing in anything. Your boyfriend is a lucky guy."

I smirked at him, letting him know I'd caught his intention. "I don't have a boyfriend, Blake."

"Good." He stuck out his hand. "Which means there's no one to object if I ask you to dance, right?"

I managed a smile, forcing myself not to look over at Jax.

"I promise I won't step on your toes," he said, grinning.

I chuckled. "With you, Blake, I can't be too certain. You dumped beer on me, remember?"

Amusement filled his face. "You're not going to let me live that down, are you?"

"Never," I replied, slipping my hand in his and allowing him to lead me to the dance floor.

He stopped on the edge of the dance floor and reached for me, wrapping his hands around the small of my waist. I stepped closer to him and caught the scent of his perfume, waiting for it to make me swoon. It didn't. As we swayed, my gaze met with Jax's, and I almost froze from the deadly fury in his eyes. I didn't want to hurt Blake's feelings, so I kept going instead of making a beeline toward Jax I wanted. The way Jax stared at us, like he wanted to rip us into pieces... it made me so hot. So horny. I could barely contain myself.

My heart danced in my chest when I saw him approaching us. I faltered, stepping on Blake's feet. He played it off with a laugh and continued, but it wasn't for long. Jax stopped right in front of us, and it surprised me how calm he seemed now.

"Ms. Reynolds– a word," he said, his voice deep and firm.

Blake pulled away and stepped back, looking like he'd been caught with his hand in a cookie jar.

"Mr. Madden," he said quickly. "We were just dancing—"

"Ms. Reynolds," Jax interrupted, not acknowledging Blake, his eyes fixed on me.

"Sure," I said, glancing at Blake, knowing my emotions were stamped on my face. "I'll be right back, okay?"

Blake quickly nodded, his face beet red. "Yeah, sure... no problem."

Jax had already walked off, cutting through the crowd of people like they weren't there. It felt like I was being called into the principal's office; well, if the principal was over six feet tall with a hot body that I wanted to climb so much. I followed him out of the main hall and around the side of the building, where it seemed deserted. My libido didn't miss how private it was.

He stopped and turned abruptly, and I almost bumped into him, the deep scowl on his face not surprising me at all.

"What are you doing?" he grounded out, his jaw clenched so tight I could see the muscles working up in his jaw.

"Huh?" I asked.

"You heard me."

"And clearly, I don't understand what you mean," I threw back, not liking his tone, especially after our earlier conversation.

"I invited you here," he said, his eyes firmly planted on me.

"You did."

"That means you should be at my side, not gallivanting on the dance floor. You're not here for that," he said.

I shot up a brow. "I didn't get the memo. Besides, you were the one who walked away from me, not the other way around."

Jax sighed harshly, raking his hand through his hair, disturbing the neat arrangement. He mumbled something unintelligible, the tension making his body stiffer than usual.

"Is that it?" I asked. "Can I go back to my dance partner?"

"Over my fucking dead body," he blurted.

"It's just a dance. That's not against company policy."

"I don't care. You're not going to dance with Kinley. In fact, I forbid you to make him touch you again."

"You can't do that. I'm a grown woman—"

He gripped my arm, the move so sudden it made me gasp. "Don't try me, Alyssa. I don't want Kinley's hands on you. Ever."

"Why not?" I pushed, knowing his intention but needing to hear him say it.

"Because you are mine!" he shouted, then caught himself, releasing me with another harsh sigh. "You are mine, Alyssa," he whispered.

I swallowed as a fluttery sensation passed through me. "You don't act like it," I said.

"Do you think this is easy for me?"

"I don't know what you want, Jax, and I'm not sure you know, either. One minute you're hot for me, and the next minute you're giving me the cold shoulder. I don't know if you're into me or if you're just messing with my head."

His jaw ticked. "I don't *mess around*," he said.

"Well, maybe you should be clearer about what you want—"

"I think that was pretty obvious the other evening in my office," he cut in.

Heat filled my body from the memory of him going down on me. "But the next day, you pretended like I didn't exist."

"Do you think it doesn't bother me to see you and can't fucking touch you the way I want to?"

I bit the insides of my lips. "You can, but you don't want to. We're only here because you got jealous of me dancing with Blake. You don't want to claim me, but no other man should, either."

"That's bullshit, and you know it."

"Then prove it. Show me how much you want me." My body trembled as I stepped up to him. "Show me, Jax."

"Fucking hell," he breathed.

"Please."

He growled softly, taking my mouth for a kiss, stroking my lips with so much passion that left my knees weak. In that moment, I didn't care who came upon us. I was so caught up in the pleasure from his skillful mouth that only a natural disaster could break us apart. I'd spent days wondering if this would ever happen again. There were times I doubted it would, but here we were, like fire and ice; me burning, him thawing out, both desperate for each other.

He cupped my face with his hands and pulled away slightly, his harsh pants telling me how much the kiss affected him, too.

"Let's get out of here," he said, his voice low and husky.

I swallowed, searching his face, knowing exactly what he meant. "Are you sure?"

He nodded, giving us some distance. "Meet me in the parking lot in five," he said before he stepped away and headed back to the banquet hall. I willed myself to calm down, smoothed out my dress and then walked to the bathroom to fix my smudged lips and re-arrange my fuzzy hair. I studied myself in the mirror, seeing the excitement in my eyes, the flushness on my cheeks and the way my nipples pressed against the fabric of my dress. Hoping no one would notice how aroused I was, I returned to the main hall.

I spotted Blake at the bar sipping a martini and talking to a girl our age. He turned and saw me, a flash of guilt moving across his face, but I gave him a reassuring smile. I didn't care that he'd found someone else to talk to. In fact, it made me feel less guilty about leaving him alone.

"Everything okay?" he asked after introducing me to the cute redhead. Her name was Sasha, and she was obviously into him.

"Um... yeah. I have this thing to take care of for Mom – listen, I'll see you on Monday, okay?" I couldn't help the lie. If he noticed Jax had gone missing, he might connect the dots. I didn't want our secret coming out, not when Jax had just opened the door.

Blake pulled me into a brief hug. "Get home safe, okay?"

"Definitely."

I gave Sasha a departing smile, then left the banquet hall. When I got to the parking lot, there was no sign of Jax, but I didn't have to worry for long. Headlights blinked on my right, and I checked my surroundings before moving briskly to his car.

A sudden ball of nervousness lodged itself at the bottom of my gut as I slid onto the leather seat of his luxury ride. I took a deep breath, glancing over at him and seeing the concern on his face.

"Are you sure you want to do this?" he asked.

"Of course, I'm sure," I replied. "Are you?"

"I've never been surer of anything in my life, Alyssa."

Holy shit. A faint smirk formed on my lips as Jax pulled out of the parking lot, speeding off into the night.

Chapter 15

Alyssa

Jax Madden's home reminded me of those luxury condos I'd seen on HGTV, shaped like a fancy cube with more emphasis on symmetry than anything else. The interior had a crisp, masculine decor, mostly black and white colors, which did not surprise me, knowing who Jax was.

I followed him down a long hallway with oil paintings on either side; then we stepped into the living room, where floor-to-ceiling windows illuminated the huge space. There were plush, snow-white couches huge enough to hold a baseball team with a coffee table between them. A large TV stood against the wall, covering most of it. An abstract black and white rug covered the entire floor.

"Can I get you anything to drink?" Jax asked, removing his jacket and carefully laying it across the back of the couch.

"Um... water is fine," I replied. I wanted to have my wits about me. Jax Madden was about to make love to me, and I wanted to remember every second of it.

I moved around the room after he left for the kitchen to fill my order, taking in the photos against the mantel. A photo of him smiling caught my eye. He looked so weird that it made me laugh. I giggled, reaching for it, observing the older woman next to him, his spitting image. His arm lay protectively around her shoulders, and it was obvious they both got the joke.

"My mom," his sudden voice came from behind me, making me jump.

I gasped as the photo fell from my hands. Luckily for me, it didn't break.

"Sorry." I reached to the floor, but he beat me to it, straightening as he stared at the photo with a fond smile.

"She's beautiful."

I glanced up at him, the tenderness still there. "She's my world." He returned the photo to its place with a soft sigh. "My motivator. She single-handedly raised me after my father disowned us, and I promised to make it worth her while. I promised to make her proud of me."

I glanced around the exquisite living room. "Seemed like you did that and more."

He nodded. "Yet, it doesn't feel enough."

His response puzzled me enough to comment, "Are you kidding me? You're a freaking billionaire."

Jax smiled and shook his head. "When you're as successful as I am, you'll understand."

His obvious faith triggered a smile that made my cheeks hurt. "Do you really think that's possible for me?" I asked.

"As long as you want it, then yes, it is. You're a smart woman, Alyssa. You maintained a decent average in high school despite missing half your classes, then you skyrocketed in college, making the honor roll every year. There's no doubt in my mind that you can do great things."

I took a drink of water, too caught up with emotions to reply. Besides my mom, no one had ever expressed such faith in me before. It touched me deeply. "Thank you for saying that," I finally replied.

"It's the truth," he replied.

I glanced back at the photo, remembering something he'd said earlier. "You mentioned your dad disowning you. Do you mind telling me what happened?"

A dark cloud immediately formed on his face, and I regretted the question at once. I expected him to brush me off with a curt response, but he breathed a soft sigh.

"My mother was his mistress; only she didn't know until she got pregnant with me. When she told him about the pregnancy, he wanted her to get rid of it. She refused, and he left her to raise me on her own."

"Oh, my God," I replied, palming my cheeks, pity filling me.

"Don't feel sorry for me, Alyssa. I'm successful today because he abandoned me. I put every effort into rising to the top to make him see how much I accomplished without his help. Now that I have, I want to knock him off his high horse. Acquiring Stag was my first step. Once I get it out of the red, I'm going for him."

"But is he worth it?" I asked.

"He's not, but I have a point to prove. Even with my success, he's never acknowledged me."

"And you hope to get his attention by taking over his company," I said wisely.

Jax clicked his tongue, pointing at me. "Smart girl. I knew you were more than a pretty face."

I laughed at his joke but then got serious. "You're doing exactly what I did when my dad died, trying to run from your pain. I wasted my time doing stupid shit. You're giving your energy to a man who doesn't deserve it, energy that could be useful elsewhere."

A smirk played at the corners of his lips, and he moved toward me. "I know exactly where I can use some of the energy right now."

I frowned at his obvious attempt to deflect but melted when he pulled my body against his. "I didn't imagine getting advice from a twenty-three-year-old, but I appreciate it," he said with a tender expression, making me warm inside.

"There's plenty more where that came from," I replied.

He released me, rolling up his sleeves as he watched me, the tenderness gone, his gaze now firm. "I need you to understand this, Alyssa. What happens tonight can never leave this apartment. There will be no discussions at your little girls' night out, no entries in your diary, not even a whisper to your shadow. No one can know. Understood?"

My stomach dropped, but I forced a smile. "I don't have a diary."

He smiled briefly, then reached for me again. I thought he'd kiss me, but he just stared into my face. I trailed my hands across the hardened contours of his chest, waiting for him to make a move. My breathing paused as a caring emotion flashed across his eyes. He cupped my face, licking his lips.

"Sometimes, I wish..." he murmured but said nothing more.

He lowered his head, and I moaned when his lips met mine. This time, there was no urgency or fear of being caught. It was just me and Jax in this secret place, both ready for each other, nothing to hold us back this time.

I looped my hands around his neck and tiptoed a little, meeting his soft strokes. He held me firmly, his hands wrapped around my waist as he passionately increased the pace. Every single nerve in my body became awake, and the longer he kissed me, the more unbearable the heat between my legs.

I could still taste the faint traces of champagne on his breath, the hint of sweetness making me deepen the kiss, wanting more. He smelled like rosewood and citrus – a blend potent enough to heighten my arousal. My chest brushed against his, my nipples tight under my dress as they grew hard with my lust for him.

Effortlessly, Jax found the zipper at the back of my dress. He pulled it down slowly, the sound almost grating in the silence. My head swirled, a gasp leaving my lips as his warm hands touched my skin. A bolt of heat blazed through me, his fingertips laced with fire as it trailed its way down my bare back.

The kiss ended, and I stood there, breathing heavily as I anticipated his next move. His grey eyes seemed darker, his ears a little red as he looked down at me before reaching for the straps on my shoulder. I held my breath, unable to take my eyes off his as he peeled them off and allowed the dress to slither to the floor. Besides the pair of lace thongs that barely covered my pussy, I wore nothing else.

Jax's eyes traveled downward, carefully drinking in every inch, pausing at my breasts, the nipples like tiny peaks. His Adam's apple bobbed, and I could clearly see the lust in his eyes as he examined me.

"How can someone be this flawless?" he muttered, his voice husky.

My cheeks warmed as a response failed me. I gasped as Jax lifted me in his arms, and I wrapped my legs around him as he carried me up the stairs, his hand resting just below my ass, my pussy pressed against his front.

He paused at the first door on the landing, and I heard a soft thud as he kicked it with his foot. I glanced around as we entered the guest bedroom. It had to be. There were no personal touchs; just snow-white furniture, random paintings, no photos at all.

I had no time to consider why he didn't take me to the master bedroom. Jax had already laid me on the bed, yanking my panties over my hips. My soaking panties. I blushed so hard when he sniffed them with a soft growl. I covered my face, suddenly too shy to look anymore. I'd never had a man smell my panties before. Jax chuckled, then he shifted my hands and captured my lips, the kiss deepening with each stroke. My body rocked as I ground my pussy against his front.

"You're trying to ruin me, aren't you?" he mumbled against my mouth.

"I'm only returning the favor," I breathed, my body quivering from how aroused I was.

He launched back, trailing his fingers down my body as he straightened. I bit my lips, watching him pull at the top buttons on his shirt, exposing his sculpted chest. Impatience took over, and I raised myself up to quicken the process, pulling the shirt off his shoulders and admiring how perfectly designed he was. I was a lucky girl. At least, that was how I felt in that moment.

Jax's pants followed suit, and I stared unflinchingly at his cock straining against his boxers, ready for every inch inside me. I pulled at the waistband, watching as his length sprung free, bobbing before it settled in a gentle bounce. He was huge, the length of him lined with veins that disappeared right before the bulbous pinkish head.

Jax stepped out of his boxers and held his cock, my small hand barely wrapped around it. Desire flooded me, giving me a mouthwatering urge to put his cock in my mouth.

He must've read my mind. His hand moved to the back of my head, gently circling, his eyes on fire with lust for me. "I want my cock in your mouth," he whispered, his body rocking as he fucked my palm. "Get on your knees for me, baby."

My pussy flooded from the order, and I dropped to my knees, my face in line with his cock. I trailed my hands along his length, admiring the soft foreskin despite him being stone hard. His pubic area was smooth and shaved, and he smelled so good.

I held the base, taking the tip in my mouth, giving it a hard suck before circling it with my tongue. Jax gripped my hair with a loud hiss, the action sending ripples of satisfaction through me. I took more of his length in my mouth, my lips gliding along the rock hard, velvety base. Jax moaned as I tightened my lips around him, slowly making my way down to the base, only managing to get halfway. I worked my up, then down again, building a steady rhythm, my hands gripping his ass.

"Fucking hell, Alyssa," Jax grounded out, both hands gripping my head as he gently fucked my mouth.

I moved further down on him, wanting to get every inch of him into my mouth. It seemed impossible, so I settled at mid-length, massaging his balls while I sucked him. His loud, harsh breaths filled the room, giving me an ego boost. For a man who was always so controlled, I enjoyed watching him fall apart for me.

He soon pulled back, breathing so hard, his tousled hair hanging over his eyes. "Jesus," he whispered, staring at me in disbelief.

I suppressed my satisfied smirk but couldn't contain my giggle as he pulled me up and kissed me hungrily, his cock poking at my stomach. He moved forward, and my legs soon pressed against the bed. As he leaned me back, I stopped him with a hold on his hand.

"I want to ride your cock," I whispered.

Jax growled, running his fingers through my hair, bringing my head back and kissing my chin. "There's nothing sexier than a woman who knows what she wants."

We switched positions, and I watched his biceps ripple as he pushed himself up on the bed, laying on his back and waiting for me to take charge. I bit my lips and climbed onto the bed as Jax stroked his cock.

"Do you think I can fit, sweetheart?" he asked, looking like a sexy devil as he lay there, his messy hair so incredibly attractive.

"You can definitely try," I teased as I straddled him, my pussy hovering above his rigid cock.

I rubbed myself against him, a shuddering moan escaping as his hardness grazed my sensitive flesh. His hands trailed over my thighs, impatience filling his eyes. I wanted to tease him a little longer, but he looked just about ready to wreck me if I kept him waiting too long.

I eased up, using one hand to hold his cock before I lowered myself on him. My eyes flew shut as I gasped, my flesh stretching to take him in. I was so wet, yet there was still some resistance as he filled me.

"Oh, my God," I exclaimed, arching my back, my hands pressed on his thighs.

Jax's jaw was clenched tight, a single vein protruding in his forehead. "Fuck, you're tight," he grunted. "I don't want to hurt you, baby."

"No holding back, Jax," I muttered, trying to sink deeper. "Please give me everything you've got."

Jax's eyes narrowed, and with one swift movement of his hips, he thrust inside me, and I groaned, feeling the full length of him. My mouth remained open, my body soaring to a dangerous high as his cock filled every inch of me.

I whimpered, not moving an inch as my pussy hugged him, getting used to his size. Jax eased himself into a sitting position and wrapped his arms around me. Our bodies became one, my hard nipples pressed against his chest, the sensation feeling so good.

He trailed his fingers up my back, leaving a thrill that traveled all the way up my spine. He released the pin that held half of my hair together, the thick locks tumbling down my back and around my face. Jax's eyes darkened, and I saw something there that made my heart flutter. I clung to him, tears stinging my eyes, triggered by the sudden emotions running through me.

It was so easy, too easy to fall for this man, but it wasn't the ideal thing to do. Jax was way out of my league, he was my boss, and this was only a secret fling. I tucked the reminder into the front of my mind, so I'd never forget.

I wrapped my arms around him and rotated my hips, his cock moving inside me. Heat radiated between us as we fucked each other, pleasure building with each sweet stroke. Jax kissed my neck and nibbled my shoulders, and my eyes rolled to the back of my head from the sweet and spicy pain that consumed me. He resumed his position, laying back down on the bed, watching me, his gaze unwavering as he examined my body — particularly the area where we were joined.

I arched my back again to give him a better view, my hips rising and falling as his cock moved back and forth inside me, each deep thrust breaking me down, making me fall harder for him.

Oh, boy.

Chapter 16

Jax

Perfect.

The only word to describe this moment. Alyssa in my bed, her soft body on top of me, her tight little pussy gripping my cock, the soft moans that left her lips, the sweet scent of her body mixed with the intoxicating scent of our lovemaking... should I go on? There were no flaws. No complaints. I didn't want this moment to end.

Alyssa was a bad girl trying to be good. I realized that from the first day that she entered my office. I sensed her passion from the way she came on to me, the way she responded when I ate her out. There was no doubt she would be good in bed, never boring. But even knowing that, her wildness in bed still surprised me. She was a firecracker, fucking me so hard and skillfully, leaving me in awe.

My cock was lathered in her sweet cream as I glided back and forth inside her like a piston in her tight pussy, her lips feathering back and forth with each thrust while her cream trailed to the base.

Her hair bounced softly with each movement, matching the jiggling of her breasts. I gripped her waist as I spread my thighs and pressed inside her, sliding in more on my length. Her walls hugged me, making me want to bust inside her, but

I held onto every bit of restraint I had. It wasn't yet time. I wanted to enjoy every moment of this.

"Oh, yes, Jax; I love how you feel inside me," she gasped, eyes closed, her tits bouncing, her nipples erect and pebbled.

I flipped her over, loving the sexy groan that escaped her lips. I eased over her, acknowledging how beautiful she looked lying there, her hair sprawled out against the pillows, her lips slightly swollen from kissing. A sudden rush of affection made me stroke her cheeks, then I pulled back, reminding myself this was only a fling. I didn't want to get too deep with someone who was out of bounds.

I pried her legs further apart, exposing her pussy. She moaned when my fingers teased her clit. "Keep doing that, Jax," she whispers. "It feels so fucking good."

Pushing up on my knees, I gave her pussy my full attention, pulling back the hood on her clit and licking the most sensitive spot. Alyssa bucked, her loud gasps filling the room.

"Jax!" she breathed.

The tip of my tongue flicked against the hard knob, gently teasing, then picking up the pace, slowing down, then going hard again.

"Don't stop... don't stop... give me more, Jax. Yes... fuck. Fuck!"

Hearing the filthy sounds from her mouth left me so hard, on the verge of an explosion. After licking her to a sheet-pulling orgasm, I thrust into her, almost driving to the hilt. She screamed as her pussy hugged my cock, her head thrashing, her slender hands molding her breasts as I slammed into her, my thrusts more fluid with each stroke. Within minutes, I was effortlessly gliding inside her, the squelching sounds of her pussy turning me on even more.

Determined to give her another earth-shattering release, I found her clit, massaging it with my thumb as I drilled her with every force I could muster. Alyssa was a mess beneath me; eyes rolling over, fingers gripping the sheet until her knuckles whitened, sweat running down her face like a river.

"What are you doing to me?" she whimpered.

"The same thing you're doing to me, baby," I huffed, remembering her response earlier. We were still within the throes of passion, and I was already a ruined man. Alyssa had already stolen a piece of my soul.

"You're going to make me come," she whispered, tension lining her face.

"Yes, baby." I dug deep, and she groaned. "Come for me."

"Oh, Jax!"

The sound of my name on her lips triggered my own release. I bucked inside her, groaning deeply as we came together, her pussy pulsing around me. My warm semen filled her, marking my territory. In that moment, with my mind hazy with lust, the consequences be damned, I made my claim. Alyssa was mine.

She floated back to earth with soft whimpers, her body writhing on the bed with my cock still buried deep inside her, pouring out every drop of cum inside her. I kissed her open mouth before I pulled myself out and fell beside her, breathing heavily.

The undeniable satisfaction on her face was an ego booster. I reached for her without even thinking about it. I shouldn't cuddle, but damn, it felt so good. She snuggled up to me with a contented sigh, and a similar emotion ran through me.

"That was the most amazing experience of my life," she said, her voice low.

I smiled, pleased. "Ditto."

"Somehow, I don't believe that."

"Why?"

She turned, facing me with a slight frown. "I've seen the photos online. You're not a saint."

"Didn't say I was, but it takes nothing from the facts. This was amazing." I kissed her forehead, and her expression softened. "You're amazing."

She smiled, then settled beside me where we lay in silence until sleep beckoned to me. I was on the verge of drifting off when the mattress moved, and I opened my eyes to find Alyssa shimmying from the bed.

"Where are you going?" I asked, pushing myself up on my elbow.

She stared at me like I'd just asked a ridiculous question. "Home. It's almost midnight."

"No." I reached for her hand. "Stay with me tonight."

She looked down at me, an uncertain smile playing on her lips. She didn't how beautiful she looked being so vulnerable.

"Are you sure?" she asked.

Yes. No. I don't know. I have this sudden urge to wake up to your face every morning, yet I know it's the wrong thing to do. Out loud I replied, "Yes, I'm not ready to let you go."

Alyssa's eyes sparkled as she beamed, then she came back to cuddle with me. "FYI; I snore," she informed me with a giggle, resting her head against my chest.

Another rush of affection made me smile as I wrapped my hand around her and kissed the top of her head. Somehow, this felt perfect – natural, like Alyssa belonged exactly where she was. In my arms.

I just wished things were less complicated.

SUNDAY MORNING FOUND me out of bed—a first, feeling ten years younger and doing something very rare. Cook. I usually had brunch with a few associates, but I canceled. Since Alyssa was here and still asleep, I decided to cook, knowing she'd probably be ravenous when she woke up.

I made eggs, which were slightly burned but still edible. Bacon and toast joined the mix with some fruits I'd had delivered the other day. I carried it to the bedroom with a glass of pineapple juice, just in time to see Alyssa stirring in bed.

As if sensing my presence, she got up, her smile stirring my heart. Was this happiness? If it was, I wanted more. So much more.

"Thought you might be hungry," I said, approaching the bed and resting the tray beside her.

Alyssa tucked a strand of hair behind her head and nodded. "Starving. This was the last thing I expected. Thank you." She leaned in to kiss me softly on the lips, confirming what I'd already suspected. She was already under my skin. I would never get enough of her.

"You're welcome."

She assessed the tray and smiled. "I can't believe you did this."

"Why not?"

"I thought there would be butlers at your beck and call. I'm struggling to believe you know how to turn on a stove."

She laughed as I poked her side.

"I wasn't born with a gold spoon in my mouth, Alyssa. As rich as I am, I haven't forgotten the days when my mother struggled to put food on the table. Doing my own housework keeps me humble."

Alyssa nodded, plucking a grape from the bunch. "It's shocking as hell, but I'm impressed. It makes you seem... human."

"Are you saying I'm not human?" I asked with amusement.

A soft smirk tugged at her lips as she popped the grape into her mouth. "After last night, I'm really not sure."

For some reason, her response made me laugh.

"You should do that more," she said.

"What?"

"Laugh. It makes you more approachable."

I shook my head. "I'll pass."

She paused plucking another grape, staring at me. "I don't get it. Don't you want people to like you?"

"No."

"Why not?"

"Because I've been burned too many times by people who 'like' me," I replied, making air quotes. "I started at the bottom with many friends. Now, I'm at the top with none. I wouldn't have gotten here if I hadn't let them go."

"Oh, that's rough," she replied. "I can't imagine having no friends."

"Of course not. You're young."

She made a face. "I'm twenty-three years old. Not *that* young."

Yeah, not that young; even so, our age gap still concerned me. I pressed my hands on the bed, pushing myself forward to get up. "Enjoy your breakfast."

She grabbed my hand. "Join me."

Her smile compelled me, the sparkle in her hazel eyes also doing me in. It didn't matter how loud my instincts screamed to end things before they got too deep. One smile, one beckon of her curved finger, and I was like putty in her hands.

I rejoined her, but as I reached for a strawberry, she leaned over and kissed me, her mouth fruity and sweet, just as addicting as the first time. The lingering warning flew out of my head, banished by the feel of her soft lips, her fingers stroking my chest. I kissed her fervently, arousal heightening inside me.

The loud shrill of her cellphone pierced the air. Alyssa groaned as I pulled away.

"Whoever it is can wait," she mumbled, reaching for me again, but the sound drove a wedge between us as it kept ringing.

"It could be an emergency. Maybe you should answer it," I suggested.

With another groan, Alyssa moved away, sliding off the bed. She moved to where I'd placed her phone on the night table, releasing a curse as she stared at the screen. I watched as she hurried from the room, the sheet wrapped around her body.

Not wanting to eavesdrop on her conversation, I waited in the room, nibbling on a few berries as her muffled voice came from somewhere down the hall. I couldn't make out her words, but based on her tone, there would be no round two.

She returned a minute later, concern on her face. "It's my best friend. Apparently, she's at my house, and mom's freaking out because I didn't come in last night."

Again, that major issue became obvious, making my heart sink. Alyssa was twenty-three years old, but she still lived under her mother's roof, still a child in her mother's eyes. It didn't even occur to have her send a reassuring text last night. With the other women I'd been with, there was no need for that.

Alyssa sighed heavily. I'm sorry I can't stay longer," she said, wrapping her arms around me.

I smiled and kissed her briefly on the lips. "It's fine. I'll order you an Uber." I couldn't risk her mother seeing me if I dropped her off.

"In the meantime, I'll craft a believable lie to explain where I was last. God, it feels like I'm back in high school."

I didn't know how to respond to that, so I focused on ordering the Uber while she got ready. She slipped on her dress and backed up to me, and I zipped her up, remembering last night when I took it off. I ignored the stirring in my groin when my fingers brushed against her soft skin.

Down boy.

Alyssa turned to me with a smile, trapping her hair behind her ear. "I had an amazing night, Jax."

"So did I," I replied. It was the truth. Whatever happened beyond today, I'd never forget how special it was.

"See you at work tomorrow."

I nodded and managed a smile, and before I knew it, the house was silent again. It sucked, but that phone call had only proven one thing: I had only fooled myself into thinking this would work. It wouldn't.

Chapter 17

Alyssa

My hand hesitated on the knob of my front door before I pushed it open. I saw Liz's car outside, which confirmed she was still there. I wished she'd called to let me know about dropping by. If she had, I wouldn't be in this mess. Back in high school, Liz had always been my alibi when I slept over at a guy's house. In fact, she would've been my cover today. Last night wasn't planned, so it didn't occur to give her a heads-up; now, it left me fumbling with a proper lie. I wasn't a kid anymore, but I couldn't tell Mom where I really was last night. I couldn't bear her disappointment in me, especially when I'd redeemed myself so well.

As I stepped inside, I heard their chatter in the living room, so I moved in that direction. Their heads turned as I approached, Liz wearing a knowing smirk, relief filling Mom's face.

"Hey, guys," I said, managing a tight smile.

"Oh, sweetie, thank God you're okay," Mom said, rising from the couch and coming to me. "I almost lost my mind when Liz showed up, and you were nowhere in the house, and your car parked out front." She looked me over, taking in my rumpled hair. "Where have you been?"

Behind her, Liz mouthed a 'Sorry,' and I grimaced in reply.

"I was out with a friend, Mom," I replied. "I'm sorry about not calling, I um... I got caught up. But as you can see, I'm perfectly fine."

She scowled. "I hope he's not some random you met last night. Alyssa, those days are over. You're better than that."

It was no use denying I'd been out with a guy. Not when I looked like this. "He's not a stranger," I replied, hoping my response wouldn't bite me in the ass. "Can I go now?"

"Is he someone I know?" she queried.

"I almost bit my tongue with the lie. "No. Someone from high school."

"Oh. I hope he's not one of those dumb jocks you messed around with back then. Did he at least take you home? And why didn't you drive to the event last night?"

"Jeez, Mom! Quit with the third degree, please!" Liz looked so uncomfortable, which made me embarrassed. "I'm not a kid anymore. I'm twenty-three years old. With all due respect, I don't have to explain anything to you."

Mom's face reddened, but she said nothing more. I turned on my heels and headed upstairs, a lump forming in my throat. Liz's footsteps sounded behind me, but I didn't look back until I reached my bedroom door.

"That outburst was totally uncalled for," she scolded me, her expression stern.

I sighed. "I know." My mom and I hadn't butted heads in years, and I hated how terrible it made me feel. "I'll apologize to her later."

"You'd better," Liz warned as I opened the door.

"Why didn't you tell me you were coming over?" I asked.

"I'd been texting you all morning, but you didn't answer, so I drove over, assuming you were still hungover or something. I didn't think you'd be shacked up with your boss – least of all this late. It's almost midday."

My eyes widened, and I covered her mouth to shush her. "Wha– how did you know where I was?"

Her eyes sparkled with humor. "Wild guess. You just confirmed it." I pushed her shoulder, and she giggled. "I told you he couldn't resist you in that dress."

I bit my lips, my cheeks warming at the memory of last night. "I didn't even realize it was so late."

Liz came to sit beside me on the bed. "Sounds like you had the night of your life."

I plopped on my back, breathing out a deep sigh. "It was amazing, Liz. I can't even put it into words."

Liz clapped her hands. "Details. I want details!"

I smiled. "He's a totally different person from that grumpy boss in the office," I told her. "He even made me breakfast in bed."

Liz swooned. "Oh, that's so sweet! So, are you guys a thing?"

"A secret thing," I replied, then proceeded to tell her about the company policy.

She palmed her cheeks with a groan. "No! That's total BS. Who made that stupid policy?"

"Jax did."

"Oh, damn. Talk about a plot twist. At least you know what his intentions are."

"Do I?"

She stared at me oddly. "Duh. He only wants pussy. That man will never claim you as his woman."

Her words made my stomach drop, but I answered calmly. "That's okay. I'm not looking to get claimed, either. I'm a free spirit."

"I thought you wanted to be a Stepford Wife." She tapped her chin, looking upwards. "What were your exact words? 'I want to find a decent man and settle down. No more running around for me.'"

"It's not a crime to change my mind, is it?"

"Of course, it's not." She held my shoulders, staring into my face. "You know me. I'm all for living your best life but don't compromise who you really are, Ally. You're not the girl you were in high school, and quite honestly, I'm glad." She winced at me. "I didn't like that girl sometimes."

"Ouch."

"Don't get me wrong, I loved you to bits, but I hated your dark side. We were all rebellious kids, but you took it up a notch."

"Way to wait five years to tell me this," I replied, shrugging her off, unable to hide how offended I was.

"We were kids, Ally. None of us thought so deeply back then. Besides, you had a wake-up call and turned over a new leaf. No harm done. Just don't go back to being that girl. Please."

I sighed, seeing her valid point. "I won't."

"Good. Now, if you want to have fun with your little grumpy boss, go right ahead. Don't fall for him, though."

"And if I do?"

Liz shook her head. "Ally, don't even think about it. Just get some good dick and keep your heart guarded. You can't fall in love with your boss— a man who's twice your age and already has life figured out. It won't end well if you do."

"Roger that," I replied with a mock salute, forcing a smile.

Later on, after Liz left, I spent the rest of the afternoon getting my outfits ready for the new week, our conversation on my mind.

"Don't fall in love with your boss," she said. *"It won't end well for you."*

Oops.

Too late.

I'D JUST GOTTEN OUT of the shower that evening when Mom knocked on the door and popped her head in a second later. "Can I come in?" she asked.

"I mean, it's your house," I murmured.

She sighed, entering. "Honey, I didn't mean to interrogate you like that earlier. I was just worried about you," she said, sitting on the edge of the bed.

I joined her. "I understand, Mom. I should have texted or called to let you know I wasn't coming home. It was the responsible thing to do."

She placed a hand on my leg. "Although you're no longer a baby, I'll always worry about you no matter what. When you have your own kids, you'll understand. You're the one and only thing that kept me going after your dad died, although you gave me hell—"

"And I can't express how sorry I am for being such a brat. I cringe whenever I think about those years."

"Honey, you've made up for it and so much more. I only ask that you make good decisions from now on, okay? I just want you to be safe."

I smiled, leaning against her. "I will, Mom."

"So, who's the guy? Is it Blake?" she suddenly asked.

I chuckled. "You're not letting that go, are you?"

"You know I won't, honey."

"I can't tell you, but it's not Blake — company policy, remember?"

"Oh, that stupid thing." She huffed. "I get that the company image has improved since that policy went in place, no sexual lawsuits and whatever, but it's just so cold to me. Imagine meeting the love of your life and having to choose him or your job."

"Yeah, imagine," I replied dryly, thinking of Jax.

She pulled in a breath and patted me on the shoulder. "Well, whenever you're ready to talk about this new guy, I'm here," she said, getting up to leave.

I didn't reply, just watched her go, my mind in turmoil. Me and Jax's affair had a limited shelf life, but if I didn't guard my heart, it could get really complicated.

But there was a slight problem. No, a huge one. I had nothing to protect my heart.

Chapter 18

Alyssa

Excited steps brought me to my workspace early Monday morning, and I glanced at Jax's office door as I placed my bag on the desk. He was already in; I saw his car parked in the reserved spot when I drove in earlier. I couldn't wait to see him, to confirm that what we shared on Saturday night wasn't a figment of my imagination. It still felt surreal.

I sat at my desk, tucking a lock of my hair behind my ear, having decided to let it loose today. After realizing Jax had liked seeing my hair worn down, I decided to give him a little gift. I had an ulterior motive, too. My fantasy of having him fuck me from behind on his desk was still alive and raging, and I wanted it fulfilled, hopefully, today.

An hour passed, and there was still no sign of him. I didn't want to intrude by knocking on his door without good reason. Good, professional reason. Jax and I had an affair, but that didn't change the dynamics of our professional relationship. He was still my boss.

Around midday, and at the brink of my impatience, the office phone rang, and my heart raced when I saw his extension on the screen. I quickly lifted the handle, placing the phone to my ear.

"Ms. Reynolds, my office, please," he said tightly, hanging up before I got a word in.

I fetched my tablet and stood, nervously smoothing out my skirt as I headed to his office. His tone did not comfort me at all. Was this another flip-flopping moment? I didn't appreciate his hot-and-cold behavior one bit.

I knocked once before I pushed the door open, finding Jax at his desk, his gaze buried in his work, his reading glasses perched above his nose. He removed his glasses as I closed the door, resting them on the desk and pinching the bridge of his nose before looking up at me.

"Hi," I said, sounding almost breathless from how nervous I was. Did he summon me to end our fling? Did he regret making love to me?

"How did it go with your mom?" he asked, and I blinked, not expecting that question.

"Um – fine. She was a bit worried, but that's about it." There was no need to give him more details.

He nodded, pulling back his chair, his powerful body rising as he stood. I swallowed hard, my pulse tripping as he moved around the desk, stopping in front of me.

"You wore your hair down," he murmured, running his fingers through it, his other hand stroking my cheek. With a sigh, I leaned into his palm, an instant desire filling me.

I wanted to tell him I did it for him, but his lips were on mine in the next moment, the soft strokes of his tongue short-circuiting my brain. With hands on his biceps, I kissed him back just as hard, just as needy, showing how much I wanted this.

Still nibbling my lips, Jax deftly unbuttoned my blouse, revealing my lace bra. I threw my head back with a deep sigh when he licked between the cleavage, then pulled back the edge of my bra, exposing my erect nipple. My breathing hitched when he nipped it with his teeth; once, twice, again and again, leaving goosebumps on my skin.

He exposed the other nipple, giving it the same treatment, making me moan his name so loud, I feared the sound would travel. I bit my lips, suppressing the moans, my body growing tense from bottling them up.

A sudden rapping on the door made me gasp, and I pulled away, staring at Jax with alarm. He silently instructed me to button my top, and I quickly obeyed, my trembling fingers slipping the buttons through the wrong holes before I realized my mistake and started over.

"Hurry!" Jax hissed, aggressively running his hand through his hair as the knock came again.

With my nerves in shambles, I finished, smoothing down my collar and patting down my hair. Jax handed me the tablet and pointed to the chair, and I rushed to sit.

"Come in," he called gruffly.

The door opened a second later, and it surprised me to see Blake enter. His smile faltered when he saw me, a slight frown on his face as he turned his attention to Jax.

"Sorry to interrupt, Mr. Madden. Mrs. Reynolds wants your approval on these latest upgrades asap," Blake said, handing Jax a file, and I didn't miss the stiffness in his tone. I glanced down at myself, double-checking that all my buttons were in place, satisfied that they looked fine. Still, I couldn't help wondering if he'd noticed something.

Jax took the folder, the tightness on his face letting me know he'd picked up on Blake's attitude, too. Blake took one look at me, then walked out, and I breathed a sigh as he closed the door.

"Do you think he's onto us?" I asked Jax.

"I don't think. I know," he replied curtly, moving back to his chair. "Which is why we have to end this. Now."

I shot up from my seat, a painful lump forming in my throat. "On a technicality? Jax, there's no proof he knows anything. We're just assuming at this point."

"I don't know about you, but my assumptions have always been spot-on. This is not a debate, Alyssa. I'm ending this."

"Just like that." It surprised me how calm my voice was. Tears stung my eyes, but I held my composure.

Jax sighed, taking his seat. "Alyssa, there's no doubt I'm attracted to you, but it's not worth losing what I've worked for—" His eyelids fluttered as he released a loud breath. "Okay, that came out wrong."

I dared not to blink. "No, it came out exactly how you meant it, *Mr. Madden*," I said.

His jaw clenched at my formal address. "*Alyssa*, let's be rational. We both knew this wasn't a long-term thing. In the heat of the moment, we forgot the reasons it couldn't be more than a fling but let me remind you. I'm almost twice your age, and I'm your boss."

"And if you weren't my boss?" I asked, blinking back the tears.

Jax gave me a long, pointed stare. "Why do I get the feeling you wanted more than a fling?"

I stared back in silence, flicking my fingernails.

"Jesus, Alyssa," he said with a groan.

My face grew heated with embarrassment. Without another word, I turned to go. Jax caught me before I reached the door, twisting me to face him. His expression settled when he saw the tears on my face.

"I'm forty-two years old," he replied. "You should be with someone your own age, someone who'll share your interests, a guy young enough to keep up with you. I'm not the one, Alyssa, and if you want to keep working here, you need to get that through your head."

I flinched from his harsh response, then I nodded, easing away from his grasp. "Understood, Sir."

His eyes searched my face; then he shook his head with a deep sigh. "You may go."

I moved off before the entire order left his mouth, heading straight to the ladies' room, where the tearful dam burst the instant I closed the door. Embarrassment, devastation and anger raged through me as I quietly sobbed, my arms wrapped around me and my forehead resting against the wall.

Chapter 19

Jax

"Only God knows why you insist on doing the dishes by hand when there's a perfect dishwasher right beside you," Mom grumbled, coming into the kitchen with a stack of plates from our just-concluded dinner.

I took the dishes from her with a wry smile. "You already know, Mom. I like getting my hands dirty. Besides, washing dishes is a therapeutic chore."

"You want something that relaxes you? Get a massage. Take a vacation. You can afford it."

"You're missing the point."

"No, I'm not." She poked my chest. "What I'm saying is, you work too hard, Jax, and I don't understand why. You have more money than you can spend in this lifetime."

"It's not about the money," I replied, squirting soap on a plate.

"Then what is it about? Power?"

At my silence, she scoffed loudly. "What use is power when you're not happy? Why do you want it, anyway?"

I paused amid sponging the plate, staring through the French windows at the garden view. I bought my mom this place when I first became a millionaire, one of the proudest moments of my life. The memory of the joy on her face had been a fuel over the years. I relied on it so much, especially when things got rough. But even after all I'd achieved, and how proud I made my mom, there was always a void she couldn't fill.

"I'm chasing the ultimate power, Mom," I said firmly, placing down the plate and turning to face her. "Because it's the only way he'll finally notice me."

A pained expression filled my mother's face, and she reached out to stroke my arm. "Oh, sweetie…" She sighed. "This may sound harsh, but it's been forty-two years. Your father might never notice you. Don't waste the rest of your life chasing someone who's not worth a minute of your time."

Tears stung my eyes as she pulled me into her arms, my chin resting on her shoulder as I reflected. Twenty-two years ago, I decided to work my butt off and get to the top where I could be my father's equal, where he'd have no choice but to acknowledge who I was. But even after all my achievements, and after we moved in the same circle, he never noticed me, never claimed me as his son.

So many years, so many hours being obsessed with one man, and what did it get me? Sure, I had money, I had influence, but was I truly happy?

No.

For twenty-two years, I'd been on autopilot, at least until a month ago when Alyssa walked back into my life, entering my office with those big doe eyes that contradicted the firecracker she was inside. She made me feel alive. For the first time in years, I looked forward to going to work, and my day wasn't made until I saw her. I told myself it was only an attraction to a beautiful woman, but I'd dated many over the years. No woman had ever given me the urge to make them spend the night. I experienced such contentment waking next to her that morning, and I craved more. This was more than an attraction. Alyssa Reynolds had gotten deep under my skin.

Mom eased me away, staring into my face. "Let him go and move on. You're still young. Use your precious time to find the happiness you deserve."

I nodded, her advice sinking in. "I will, Mom."

She smiled fondly, squeezing my shoulder before moving to the sink and taking over the dishes. "Speaking of happiness, when are you going to ask Sarah on a date? She seemed quite into you at dinner."

Making a mental note to decline any dinner invitation that involved Mom's matchmaking attempts, I shook my head in response.

"Are you serious?" she exclaimed. "Why won't you ask her out?"

"Do you have all day? It's a long list of reasons," I replied.

"This isn't the time to be picky, Jax. I'm serious about grandkids, and it's quite challenging for women in your age group to have children. Get a move on, pronto."

"Even if I wanted kids, which I'm still not sure of—" Mom gasped, and I gave her a deadpan stare. "—Sarah isn't the one. I don't want a superficial woman in my life."

"Then what are you looking for?"

"Someone who doesn't care about my wealth, for instance. I want a woman who's not afraid to be real with me, works hard, and yet knows when to let her hair down. I'm looking for a woman who makes me smile, who makes me feel.... alive."

Mom patted my back. "I wish you luck finding that unicorn, especially with how popular you are. Women look at you and see dollar signs. There's no running away from that."

"I beg to differ," I muttered, and she waited for me to elaborate, but I didn't. It just occurred to me that Alyssa ticked every item on that list, which was crazy. How can a woman out of bounds be the right one for me?

ALYSSA REPLIED IN A cool tone when I greeted her in passing, her gaze locked to the screen in front of her. Her response didn't surprise me. She'd been distant, very professional since I ended our affair last week. Guilt gnawed at my insides whenever I remembered her trembling lips, heaving chest, and the devastation so clear in her eyes. I hurt her, and I disliked myself for doing that. All I wanted to do was make it right, but until then, I'd leave her alone. I'd keep things professional.

I entered my office, the first task of the day already on my mind. After powering up my computer, I dialed an extension and delivered an order. For the next five minutes, I read through my emails until he showed up.

At his knock, I called for him to enter. Blake Kinley stepped inside, uncertainty on his face. He greeted me, and I gestured to the seat in front of him, arranging a poker face.

After Alyssa ran from my office last week, I invited Kinley back for a meeting and allowed him to present his invention to me. At first, my intention was to hear him out, hoping it would be enough to muzzle him. As his presentation went on, I realized he'd been sitting on a potential groundbreaking product, one that could turn the company around. I took the information and presented it to the board. Now I invited him to my office to deliver the good news.

I cleared my throat, staring directly into his eyes. "As promised, I gave your presentation to the board of directors last Friday, and they have approved funding of the prototype."

Kinley jumped from his seat with a shout, then caught himself and sat back down. "Oh, thank you, Sir. I—I don't know what else to say."

"Say you'll work your ass off getting it ready; that's all I ask," I replied.

He nodded vigorously. "Of course, Mr. Madden. I won't let you down."

I gestured to the door, and he got up at once, the door softly clicking behind him. I turned on the camera feed, watching as he stopped by Alyssa's desk, seeing the excitement on her face as he gave her the news. She got up and gave him a quick side hug, then sat back down. It didn't make me jealous. She wasn't into Kinley. Alyssa Reynolds only had eyes for me.

I had one aim, and it was next on my lift, to fix things before she had eyes for someone else.

Chapter 20

Alyssa

Misery followed me all the way home after work, weighing down my shoulders as I entered the front door and walked past my mom on the couch after barely greeting her. From the corner of my eye, I saw her twist in the seat, watching as I climbed the stairs. If I knew my mother—and I did, an enquiry would soon follow, so I braced myself for it, my mind already creating an excuse for my sullenness.

A week had passed since Jax—Mr. Madden ended our affair; a week since I tried convincing myself it was for the best, that I didn't need a man to feel good, that Mr. Right was out there waiting for me, blah, blah, blah—none of it made me feel better. I wanted more of him, not any other man. It hurt that his feelings weren't the same. He walked past me each day with such nonchalance as if he didn't just rip my heart to shreds. Why did I think he even cared a little for me?

That night when we made love was so magical. It wasn't just about the sex; it was the way we connected during our conversation when I saw his human side. I saw a man I could love, someone who could love me back. He wasn't the icy boss but someone with a tender side and a heart of gold. The person who dropped the stack of files on my desk earlier today was a far cry from the man who cuddled up to me that night. I resented Mr. Madden for his behavior at the office, but Jax had stolen my heart with his affection. It was such a pity they were the same.

It was one and a half months before my contract ended, but I seriously considered breaking it. I couldn't bear seeing him in the office every day, being treated to his icy demeanor, as if I didn't give him such a precious part of me. There were plenty of vacancies in the city, so I wouldn't be out of a job for too long.

After spending an hour online searching the job sites, I took a shower and slipped into loose shorts and a tank top, then debated whether I was ready to face dinner and Mom's thorough questioning. She knew me too well, and I didn't know if my excuse of a terrible headache would explain my moodiness earlier.

My stomach growled, prompting me to throw caution to the wind, and I headed downstairs to help her with dinner. She paused amid chopping carrots as I entered, her lips in a tight line. I moved to join her, and she wordlessly slid the cutting board toward me, and I took over the carrots while she washed lettuce in the sink.

"Ugh, today was hell," I began, slicing the carrot. "I have such a terrible headache. Who knew basic filing would be so hard?"

No response.

I turned, watching her vigorously wash the lettuce. "Mom?"

Mom paused, took a deep breath, then faced me, her eyes wide and searching. "What's going on between you and Mr. Madden?" she asked.

I gaped at her. "Huh?"

"Don't stand there looking dumb, Alyssa. And don't try to deny it, either. You had me fooled, thinking you've changed, but you're still determined to embarrass me, aren't you?"

"Mom—"

"How could you? He's our boss! Do you know how terrible things would be for us if this gets out? What were you thinking?"

Shame filled me. I relaxed my grip on the knife, asking quietly. "How did you know?"

"Kinley made it slip that he caught something between you and Mr. Madden the other day." At my gasp, she raised her palm. "Luckily for you, there was no one else around, and he promised not to say a word. Now, answer me. What's going on with you two?"

A lie lingered on my lips, but I brushed it away with a sweep of my tongue. The disappointment in Mom's eyes compelled me to be honest.

"We– we slept together," I said, my voice low as I watched the absolute horror that marred my mother's face.

She swallowed and shook her head, her eyes shifting as if putting the dots together. "Was he– when you spent the night–"

"Yes," I softly said, lowering my head.

"Wha– it has been what? Two weeks? How ..." she trailed off. "Jesus, Alyssa."

"I'm sorry, Mom, things just kind of ... happened."

She blinked a few times and crossed her arms. "I don't even know what to say – I've never felt so disappointed in my entire life, Alyssa."

My eyes stung with tears as I took an uncertain step toward her, but seeing her scowl, I stepped back. "Mom, that wasn't my intention. I'm so sorry. Please believe me."

She shook her head. "What did you hope to achieve in the long run? A relationship?"

"I don't know, Mom. I wasn't thinking that far ahead—"

"That's it right there," she said, pointing at me. "You weren't thinking. Even if our company allowed office relationships, this would be no more than a fling. Jax Madden isn't the settling down kind, honey. I don't want to sound harsh, but you're just another notch on his belt. I hate this for you."

I swallowed the painful lump in my throat, knowing she would hate what I was about to say even more. "I have feelings for him," I whispered, flicking my fingers against my thighs.

Mom scoffed. "Christ."

A sob escaped, then another, until my body rocked from an overflow. Mom rushed to me, enveloping me in her arms, which made me cry even more.

She squeezed me tightly. "He ended the affair, didn't he?"

I nodded on her shoulder, sobbing harder.

"Oh, sweetie... listen, you're going to find the man who's just perfect for you, but until then, just have fun. Enjoy your youth. Before you know it, you're forty-five years old with a rebellious teenager and no time to even scratch your head."

She leaned back with a smile, wiping my cheeks. Her wise words should make me feel better, but my inside still hurt. I figured things would hurt for a while, at least, as long as Jax and I shared the same space.

"Thanks, Mom." I leaned in and gave her a huge hug. "And I'm sorry for disappointing you."

"Already forgiven, honey. Just be careful from now on, okay? Stay away from Mr. Madden unless it's work related."

I promised her I would, and as we resumed making dinner, I made a promise to myself to do everything in my power to get over Jax Madden.

OVER THE NEXT WEEK, I spent my evenings applying for jobs online, with Jax's daily behavior fueling me. Granted, I noticed he wasn't as cold as before, and I even got a smile when I submitted the expense report half an hour earlier than usual, but that changed nothing. His rejection still hurt. Based on his track record, I knew he'd already moved on to the next willing victim, and even thinking about him with another woman made me want to cry. I hate being so caught up with a man. Resigning was the only solution. Out of sight, out of mind.

Well, maybe not.

I thought about him so often after our first encounter in his hotel room, and we hadn't even been physical. Imagine now, after he'd left such a mark on me. I'd never forget him.

On Thursday, I got a call from an investment firm for a job interview, and I took my lunch break on Friday to attend. By the end of day, they called me back to announce I'd gotten the job. Instead of jumping for joy, I burst out crying after I hung up the phone. I quickly wiped my face when I heard Jax's door open, arranging a smile as he approached my desk. His hands were empty, which I found odd since he only stopped by my desk when he had work for me.

"What's wrong?" he asked, surprising me. It wasn't like him to check on me at all.

"Nothing. I'm fine, Sir." I caught the annoyance on his face before I directed my attention to the computer screen.

I expected him to move away, but he didn't. My body stiffened with tension when he reached over, his fingers gripping my chin as he turned my head. "You've been crying," he murmured. "Tell me what's wrong."

"Aren't you concerned about someone seeing us?" I replied wryly, pulling back. "The company can't handle another scandal, remember?"

He sighed, straightening. "I'm concerned about *you*," he said.

"Don't be." I returned my attention to the monitor. "I'll be fine."

I listened as the patter of his footsteps moved away from me, then I breathed a deep sigh, wishing he didn't affect me so much. Getting over him would be so much easier once I left. Luckily for me, my contract did not bind me to giving two-week's notice, which meant today would be my last official day at work. My heart sank at the thought, but I pushed the sadness away. This was for the best, for Jax's sake and mine.

I spent the weekend drafting my letter, and after a nerve-racking, sleep-challenged night, I got dressed in a pair of skinny jeans and a buttoned-up shirt, opting for a semi-casual dress code. Mom had already left for work after double-checking if I had any second thoughts. She didn't want me to quit, but when I explained, she backed off trying to change my mind.

My breath paused for a beat as the elevator doors opened on the executive floor, and I braced for a confrontation. I should've asked HR to deliver his copy instead of doing it myself.

Curious stares followed me as I walked purposefully down the hallway. Not only was I an hour late, but my jeans pants did not fit the company dress code. News of my resignation would soon surface. I only hoped they did not find out why I left.

My pace slowed when I saw Blake standing in front of Jax's office door, his face lighting up when he saw me. His expression instantly switched to curious as he looked me over. "Did I miss the memo on casual day?" he joked.

"No, you didn't. I'm here to resign."

Blake's eyes popped open. "Whoa, what?"

Not in the mood for a conversation, I gestured to the door. "Is Mr. Madden there?"

"Uh... no. I came to see him, but he's not in yet—wait a minute, why did you resign? Was it because of... you know?"

"What you let slip to my mom? No, Blake," I said evenly. "Although you shouldn't have said a word. What you did was messed up, and you know it because you've avoided me since then."

He slapped his forehead with a sigh. "I know, and I feel like shit because of it, but I didn't intend to rat you out. Still, Alyssa, you must admit that it's crazy. You and our boss—"

"Let's not talk about it, Blake," I interrupted. "What's done is done. I'm going to leave this on Mr. Madden's desk and get out of here."

Blake gave me a sad smile. "Do your thing. I'm going to miss our lunch breaks, though. I messed things up, but I truly hope we remain friends…"

I nodded, moving forward as he stepped aside. "Of course. I'll see you around, Blake."

"Oh, wait a minute. I forgot to give you the great news," he said as I turned the knob. "Mr. Madden petitioned the board, and they agreed to fund my invention."

With a genuine smile on my lips, I turned around. "Wow, that's awesome! I'm happy for you. You must be excited."

Blake grinned. "And nervous. This is a huge deal. I don't want to mess it up." His phone beeped, and he glanced at it, then backed away. "Gotta go. Your mom's wondering what's taking me so long."

He gave me a quick wave, then moved briskly down the hall, and I opened the door to Jax's office, taking a last look around the space. I placed the letter on the desk, remembering our first steamy encounter. My body came alive at the memory, and I walked around his side, running my hand over the surface where I'd been, legs spread, his tongue lapping my clit—

Oh, hell.

With a heavy heart, my body still burning, I left his office, knowing this was the end of our short-lived romance.

Chapter 21

Jax

I ended the call with my mom after turning down her invitation for another blind date. With a weary sigh, I traced my hand over my face, making a mental preparation for another hellish workday. I'd put off going to the office early, although I'd been up since five am. Not that I'd gotten much sleep last night. Like every other night, Alyssa Reynolds had been a constant presence on my mind, keeping me up way past my usual bedtime. The last few nights were even worse.

It didn't occur to me how much ending the affair would affect her. After watching her cry over the camera feed, it broke something in me. I hurt her, and I didn't hesitate to make things right. I sat down and drafted a letter to the board, requesting an amendment to the company policy. I still awaited their approval, but there was no reason for them to deny it, especially when I ensured there would be no potential issues in the future.

After thinking about what Alyssa and Mom said, I realized how many years I'd wasted chasing power instead of searching for happiness. But no more. My father could kiss my ass. Acquiring more wealth was now a thing of the past. I had more money than I could spend in this lifetime; it was time to find my soulmate to spend it with.

There was a chance I'd already found her. Only time will tell. For now, I wanted to get to know the woman who'd made me feel truly alive for the first time in my life.

ALYSSA'S EMPTY DESK was the first thing that greeted me when I entered our office space. I checked the time and confirmed it was after ten in the morning. It wasn't like her to be so late. Did she call in sick? Maybe. She'd never taken a day off, so that was fine. Still, a gnawing feeling followed me to my office, and as I closed the door and moved toward the desk, I spotted an envelope in the center, my name scrawled in Alyssa's neat handwriting.

The hell?

My jaw hardened. A sharp pain ran through me. I suspected what it was, but if I didn't touch it or read it, then I'd keep reality at bay. Still, curiosity forced me to open it, the words like a jab to my heart. She'd gotten another job offer. Holy fuck. For the entire week I'd spent dragging my feet, waiting for the board to approve before making a move, she'd been searching for a way out.

As I plopped down in my chair with a harsh sigh, there was no denying what really bothered me. It wasn't just her resignation, but what it meant. This was her attempt to get over me.

Oh, hell no. Not if I can fucking help it. There's no way I'm letting this chance at happiness slip away.

A knock sounded at the door as I reached for my phone to dial my florist's number. I put down the device, making a mental note to call him afterwards.

"Come!" I called gruffly.

I straightened in my seat as Donna Reynolds made an appearance, fury stamped on her face, an emotion I'd never seen before.

"Mrs. Reynolds, do we have a meeting?" I asked, leaning back in my chair, watching as she approached my desk, noticing her shaking hands.

She caught me staring and slipped them behind her. "No, we don't, Sir, but I need to talk to you."

"Okay... have a seat."

"I'd rather stand if you don't mind," she replied, her hands resting on the back of the chair.

I nodded, alarm bells going off in my head.

"I'm aware this may affect my job, but I don't care. I can't hold it in anymore. What you did to my daughter—used her, then tossed her aside, was so awful of you."

"Mrs. Reynolds—"

"I respected you, Mr. Madden. You're a tough boss, but you had morals. At least, that's what I thought. You're a hypocrite, and you had no right—"

"Mrs. Reynolds." There was a clear warning in my voice, but she was too upset to hear it.

"I know how you men are; pulling one minute, pushing back the next. Don't even think about contacting her again. Stay away from my daughter!"

Mrs. Reynolds whipped around and stormed toward the door. I shot up from my chair, slamming my palms on the desk, and she stopped in her tracks. Her wide eyes met my narrowed ones as she faced me again. She swallowed, lifting her chin, reminding me so much of Alyssa that my stomach flipped.

"You've had plenty to say, Mrs. Reynolds. Insubordinately, I might add. The least you can do is hear me out."

She responded with a slight nod, and I gestured to the seat in front of me. This time, she hurried to sit, and I resumed my seat.

"You asked me to stay away from your daughter, but I can't do that," I began.

Her brows furrowed, her gaze skeptical. "Why not?"

"Because I have feelings for your daughter, and I'd like to date her," I replied.

Mrs. Reynold's mouth opened and closed simultaneously until she scoffed. "You can't be serious. What about the company policy?"

I stood, her eyes lifting to meet my gaze. "It's awaiting approval as we speak. But even if the board doesn't approve, it won't stop me from pursuing her. Yes, I hurt her, but I'll do everything in my power to make it right. You can hold me to that."

She blinked a few times, her mouth opening and closing with no words coming out.

"I'm hoping she forgives me, but I'm asking for yours first," I continued.

She remained silent for a beat, her gaze planted on me, and I sensed her dilemma. Finally, she nodded. "I'll forgive you on one condition."

"Which is?"

"That you never break her heart again. If you do, you're going to answer to me, Mr. Madden. I may not be as powerful as you are, but when it comes to my daughter, I'll do whatever it takes to protect her."

I raised my palm, pressing my other hand to my chest. "I'll protect her heart with my life, Mrs. Reynolds. That's a promise."

An emerging smile brightened her face as she rose from the seat. "For your information, she's back at home. I'd get a head start on that groveling if I were you."

Chapter 22

Alyssa

"Listen, there's no reason to feel bad. You did the right thing by quitting. There's no way you could survive working in such a toxic environment," Liz said beside me on the bed. She'd driven over to comfort me when I told her what I'd done.

"You're right, but it doesn't make me feel better. I'm in love with him, Liz, and I don't know how to stop," I replied mournfully.

Liz threw up two fingers. "Two words. Shopping. Clubbing. Both are guaranteed to pull you out of your slump."

I groaned. "I just want to lie in bed and feel sorry for myself a little longer. I should have listened to you. Falling for Jax would only break my heart."

She sighed, reaching over to stroke my hair. "I'm sorry, Ally. For once, I wanted to be wrong."

"Yeah... me too."

Her cell phone beeped, and she checked the screen with a smile. "I have to go. My dad is back in town and wants to spend the day with me."

"That a good thing, right?" I asked.

"I hope so. I just want him to be more consistent with his role as my dad. No more throwing money at me to make up for not being around. Fingers crossed, this is the start of repairing our relationship."

I got up from bed and hugged her. "I'm sure it will. Thanks for coming today. I appreciate you trying to lift my spirits."

"Anytime, sweetie. Just promise me you won't spend the day moping over that dick."

"I promise."

The sound of a car outside made us break apart. We glanced at each other, wondering who it was.

"Your mom?" Liz asked.

I got up from the bed and walked toward the window. "Couldn't be. She wouldn't be home so early."

The breath hitched in my throat when I peeked through the window and saw the sleek, luxury sedan rolling into my driveway. Jax's car. My heart galloped when he got out, his eyes hidden behind a pair of dark glasses. Why was I so happy to see him?

"Okay... so this is interesting," Liz said, coming up behind me.

"What is he doing here?" I whispered.

"There's only one way to find out," Liz replied. "Although if he's only here to ask you to take your job back, I'm giving him a piece of my mind."

We watched as Jax reached into the backseat, pulling a huge bouquet. Liz gasped. "Okay, I definitely won't give him a piece of my mind."

I bit down on my lips, my heart dancing, clashing with the urge to hide in my room. "I don't know if I'm ready to talk to him – if I'm ready to see him."

I watched him walk up the driveway, and although I expected it, I still flinched when the doorbell rang, my eyes snapping toward Liz.

"It's up to you, Ally," she said.

For a short beat, I pondered what to do. My car was in the driveway, so it was no use hiding anymore. I walked downstairs with Liz following me, my heart racing so hard I wanted to pass out. The doorbell rang again, and I sunk my teeth into my lower lip, my palm sweaty from how nervous I was.

I opened the front door, and there he was, gorgeous, completely unbothered, unlike me, whose eyes were still puffy from crying so much. It made me wonder if our affair had affected him at all. I shouldn't be surprised that he was so calm. This was Jax Madden: a man of steel with a heart of ice.

"What are you doing here?" I asked, happy with the firmness in my voice.

His gaze shifted behind me, and I felt Liz brushing against my side. "Um, I better get going," she said. "Call me later?"

I nodded. "Yeah."

Liz slipped past Jax with a slight wave, and he gave her the hint of a smile. She paused beyond, her eyes running up and down his back. I couldn't suppress my smile when she gave me two thumbs up and mouthed, *He's even hotter in person!*

Jax caught my smile and turned, looking at Liz, whose eyes widened before she spun and hurried down the driveway. He turned back to me with a slight headshake, extending the bouquet to me.

"Because saying sorry isn't enough," he said. "I hope they're pleasing to you."

I took the bouquet, sniffing the sweet arrangement, suppressing my pleasure behind them. "Thank you for these."

"It's just a preview of my apology, Alyssa. May I come in?"

I hesitated, then wordlessly stepped to the side, allowing him entry. I closed the door behind us and placed the bouquet on a side table, waiting for him to speak.

He sighed, rubbing the back of my head. "I had a speech prepared; I swear. But seeing you erased every thought from my head. I've never been so nervous, Alyssa. Or terrified."

Just the tone of his voice made me want to swoon, but I straightened myself, lifting a defiant chin. "Then maybe you should go back to your precious company where you won't feel so vulnerable."

"Alyssa—" he reached for me as I moved off. I didn't pull away because I had no strength to resist him, and though I was still pissed off at his rejection, his touch soothed me.

His gaze softened, and his Adam's apple bobbed as he swallowed. "You said something to me that night, and it resonated with me. I don't want to waste my energy on people who aren't worth my time, not when there's someone I want to give it all to."

I stared at him wordlessly, my pulse rate picking up speed as I waited for him to continue.

"You, Alyssa. I'm falling for you," he said.

I didn't know what I expected him to say, but it wasn't that. My lips trembled, and my vision grew blurry with tears. "Are you for real?"

"I am for real," he said. "You're so deep under my skin."

His confession seemed so surreal. I cleared my head with a headshake. "What about the issues that stand between us? Our age difference, the company policy."

"I don't give a shit about that anymore. Not when it stands in the way of my happiness. I'm so serious, Alyssa; the only opinion that matters is yours. Well, and your mom's. I spoke to her earlier, too. I think I have her blessing."

My eyes widened. "You did?"

He nodded. "She told me you were here."

I choked on a laugh. "My mom giving you her blessing. Wow. I thought she would've wanted to castrate you or worse."

"Well, based on her expression, she came quite close. I'm standing here because she had no weapon," he replied, and I laughed out loud.

The laugh slowly subsided as his expression grew tender.

"So, what do you say, Alyssa Reynolds? Can I take you out on a date?"

"You may," I said, moving closer to him. "On one condition."

His eyes narrowed as he watched me approach. "Which is?"

I wrapped my hands around his neck and pulled him closer, pressing my forehead against his. "Show me how much you're falling for me," I whispered.

Jax groaned as I kissed him hungrily, missing the taste of his lips and the feel of his hard body against mine. He lifted me in his arms, breaking the kiss as he carried me to my room, setting me on the bed. My hand raked through his hair as he pulled at the hem of my dress and hauled it over my hips.

I busied myself with unbuckling his belt, opening the catch with one swift movement. Jax's hot mouth kissed all over my face, the heat from his lips burning me alive. I wanted him so much, I couldn't think straight.

He put me on all fours, my heart bouncing with anticipation when his cock rubbed my entrance. I held my breath and watched him from behind, his teeth clenching as he sank into me. I shrieked and dropped my head, overcome with the ecstasy that mushroomed in my belly.

My fingers curled around the sheet, his grip tight on my hips as he fucked me raw and stern, just the way I wanted it. There would be plenty of time for lovemaking later. Right now, I wanted him to wreck me. Claim me. Show me how much he ached for me, that he endured the same agony I did last week.

When we finally soared to our high and crashed back to earth, we lay curled together, our sweat mixing, our hearts beating as one. I pinched myself to confirm this wasn't a dream, then I giggled from the sting.

This was real.

Jax Madden was falling for me.

He wanted to date me.

Somehow, I'd thawed the grumpy billionaire's icy heart. The rest of our journey should be a cakewalk from now on.

Fingers crossed.

Epilogue

Alyssa
1 year later

I sucked in a breath as Jax's hot mouth traced my nipple, sending a shiver down my spine. I moaned and groped his firm ass, his cock grazing my leg. I wanted him inside of me so badly.

"Fuck me now, Jax," I whispered, trailing my fingers against his skin. "I can't wait any longer."

White-hot lust filled me, leaving me breathless and on the verge of insanity. Jax eased up with a smirk, a lock of his silver hair dangling before his eyes.

"Mhm... so greedy," he murmured huskily, shifting his position, brushing the tip at my entrance. "Tell me how deep you want my cock, baby."

"I want you to fuck my brains out. Give me everything you've got."

"Careful what you wish for," he replied, and I held my breath, my eyes fluttering when he thrust inside me. He did so effortlessly, driving right to the hilt and teasing every nerve in my body. I clung to him, bringing his face down for a kiss as he fucked me with a hard, deep, purpose.

After a year, Jax knew which spots to hit and how to drive me over the edge. I gripped his ass and urged him on, the sensation of his cock inside me so fucking good. His warm, sweaty body slid against mine, the smell of sex and soap pungent in the air.

I groaned when he moved faster, my walls clinging to him tighter. His cock swelled inside me. I raked my fingers up his back when he touched the most sensitive spot inside me. Jax grunted as my pussy gripped him in response, burying his face in my neck, his body weighing down on mine while he fucked me. I screamed out loud, unable to contain the pleasure that sailed through me. Jax slammed into me harshly and I squealed, gripping him tighter as my orgasm erupted inside me.

A spurt of his warm cum filled me before he slowed his pace, gently bucking, whispering my name. My eyes flew shut as I quivered, heat settling between us.

A sigh of contentment escaped as I came down from my high. Jax slipped out of me, and I missed his warmth, but he soon pulled me into his arms for a tight cuddle.

"If we continue like this, we're never going to leave this hotel room," I pointed out, still trying to catch my breath.

"I don't see a problem there," he said, reaching out to touch my skin, his thumb tracing over my nipple.

"Babe..." I scolded. He knew exactly what his touch did to me, especially now with my hormones racing so much.

Jax chuckled, twisting me and kissing me briefly on the lips. "You're right... we should do something fun today, apart from making love. We have six days left on our honeymoon. It's time to explore the island."

"Not before we order room service. I'm starving."

He reached over and rubbed my stomach. "That's what happens when you eat for two. Our little man already has quite an appetite."

I giggled. "I keep telling you it's a girl."

"We'll see about that when we meet Dr. Abrahams next month," he replied.

"Yep. We'll see." I placed my hand over his, tenderness running through me. It had been a whirlwind year, one filled with so much happiness I couldn't contain myself. I went back to work for Jax, and when Madeline returned from maternity break, he promoted her to another department and hired me full-time. The company policy banning office relationships got amended, but as a part of the new rule, we had to report our relationship to HR, which meant everyone knew within two days. The expected backlash didn't come, which left me relieved. Jax and I tried not to flaunt our romance, but it felt so good to hold his hand or hug him without worrying about being caught.

We progressed so fast, with Jax asking me to move in within six months, and he proposed to me a week later. He wanted us to elope, but Mom wasn't having it. Two months before the wedding, a positive pregnancy test confirmed a new addition to our family. I couldn't describe how over the moon it made us, and the wedding was even more special knowing our bundle of joy was on the way.

I eased up on the bed, leaning against the pillows as Jax ordered room service, then reached for a remote and turned on the TV. He browsed through a few channels, then stopped when he saw an AD.

He turned to me with a grin, the pride on his face making me beam. It was an AD for Stag Technologies' latest invention smart watch Jax and Blake had designed four months ago. Based on the first month's sales report, it would soon be a huge hit, joining the line of products successfully launched by the company within the last year.

Jax had achieved his goal, getting Stag Technologies out of the red and back on top where it belonged. Not that it mattered to him anymore, but the accomplishment made him proud. His father had tried reaching out for a business luncheon, but Jax declined. He no longer wanted a relationship, especially when he didn't trust the older Madden's motive. There was no use trying to form a bond anymore.

"Penny for your thoughts," he said, bringing me back to the present.

"Just thinking about the past and keeping my fingers crossed for the future," I replied. "I'm so happy my face hurts. Thank you for loving me."

"No, thank you." He joined me on the bed, wrapping me in his embrace. "For loving a cranky old snob like me."

The familiar description made me twist to look at him, and he laughed. "Your mom had too much to drink at the wedding and let it slip. I can't believe that's what you thought of me."

I laughed back. "In my defense, I didn't know who you were. Mom made you sound like an old man. But trust me," I said, rocking my butt against his front, satisfied when he groaned. "That couldn't be further from the truth."

Jax Madden tightened his hold on me. "Let me get some food in your stomach, then I'll show you how *not old* I really am."

I squealed happily as he nibbled my neck, so contented I could explode. With our painful past behind us, a lifetime of bliss ahead, I basked in the present, so grateful for the love of a man who let his guard down for me.

Pssst ... Do you enjoy reading full length novels? If yes, then I have some great *'insiders' info'* just for you, but keep this on the hush. This deal is only for readers who have at least read one of my books to the end, ok? Did you know you can have 8 of my full-length novels PLUS an extra steamy story from IZZIE VEE[1] included as a bonus, all for just **$2.99** or ***download it for free*** if you are a Kindle Unlimited or Prime Member? This amazing deal is ***over 2,100 pages***. Get this awesome deal below ^_^ ...

2

<u>CLICK HERE TO GET THE DEAL</u>[3]

---

1. https://www.amazon.com/

s?k=izzie+vee&i=digital-text&crid=31LQJTEQYT2EE&sprefix=izzie+vee%2Cdi

gital-text%2C121&ref=nb_sb_noss

2. https://www.amazon.com/dp/B0B1YTNCKQ

3. https://www.amazon.com/dp/B0B1YTNCKQ

A HOT, STEAMY COLLECTION OF AGE-GAP ROMANCE NOVELS.

List of novels inside are:

Heating Up the Kitchen - a reverse harem romance

Just Can't Behave - a forbidden, age-gap romance

Protection Details - a bodyguard, forbidden, age-gap romance

Getting Through the Seasons - a stepbrother's best friend, enemies to lovers

Getting Through the Seasons 2

Getting Through the Seasons 3

A Dose of Sunshine - a rockstar, enemies to lovers romance

Mr. Grumpy's Fake Ex-wife - a boss, stalker, enemies to lovers romance

A Bonus Novella - My Roommate's Daddy - an instalove, OTT, age-gap romance

All are standalones, contain no cheating and have happy-ever-after endings ♡

Don't miss out on this fantastic offer, grab your copy today. That's a completed 3 books series, 5 full length novels and a novella inside. **CLICK HERE**[4] to download and enjoy!

Let's connect.

Get this book for **FREE**[5] when you sign up for our newsletter. WICKEDLY STEAMY & FILTHY!

---

4. https://www.amazon.com/dp/B0B1YTNCKQ

5. https://dl.bookfunnel.com/c4j8urik87

CLICK HERE TO GET FOR FREE[6]

SAMPLE

I thought my big, over-protective stepbrother was the biggest prick ever,

Until Thanksgiving, when he brought home an even cockier devil, Sawyer,

A tattooed rebel with jawlines of steel and dark piercing eyes glinting with danger.

I can tell he's the type to fight in public brawls, someone who would protect me if I'm his,

But I'm not his type, I am too young, too inexperienced, no experience.

He has every intention of being the wicked menace to his best friend's little sister,

6. https://dl.bookfunnel.com/c4j8urik87

Hell-bent on driving me up the wall, taunting me, teasing me, torturing me, leaving me in puddles,

Yes, leaving me in puddles has become a sick little game to him,

Loving to watch me squirm in need,

Knowing damn well he'll never cross the forbidden line between us,

And my stepbrother will never let him either,

He knows Sawyer only uses shy, nerdy girls like me for a one-night stands, I know it too,

Then why do I get so weak to his tease, his touch,

I vow to myself that I will never give in to him,

My V-card will be given to a gentleman who deserves it, not a bad-ass bad boy like Sawyer,

But then I made a mistake, our lips touched ... ***DOWNLOAD FOR FREE HERE***[7].

About the Author

STEAMY, FORBIDDEN ROMANCES WITH SASSY HEROINES.

Kathilee Riley grew up in Florida and spent half of her time hating the beach and the other half daydreaming while in the sand. She's dabbled in plenty different veins of study including sociology and classic literature, but her love of steamy, forbidden romance with sassy heroines has been constant. Kathilee went from reading to writing so she could create her own worlds where love and passion bring people together, no matter their age or their differences.

Printed in Great Britain
by Amazon